OF GLASS AND ASHES

ELLE MADISON
ROBIN D. MAHLE

Of Glass and Ashes: Twisted Pages Book Three

Cover : Covers By Combs

Maps: Elle Madison

Copy Editing: Holmes Edits

Proofreading: Kate Anderson

❦

For the misfits, the forgotten, the misunderstood.
For middle children everywhere.

❦

"Acting like I'm heartless, I do it all the time.

That doesn't mean I'm scarless, that doesn't mean I'm fine."

— BISHOP BRIGGS

BONDÉ

MADAME'S ESTATE

THE HEIGHTS

KING'S SQUARE

THE HEIGHTS

MID-SECTOR

THE HARBOR

THE SLUMS

PROLOGUE
AIKA

It started the day I found out my sister died.
It started the night of the fires.

CHAPTER ONE

AIKA

*S*he's dead.

Damian's words repeat over and over in my mind, louder than Mother's screams. Louder than Damian's pleading with her for forgiveness, like a desperate, beaten hound coming back to its master.

She's dead.

Zaina is *dead*.

I try to reconcile this information, to make sense of it somehow, but I can't.

None of this makes any sense.

The sound of glass breaking pulls my attention back to the commotion in the room.

Mother's chest is rising and falling at a rapid pace, her violet eyes wide with fury and maybe pain.

I didn't know she could feel pain.

I didn't know she could feel anything.

She hurls another vase across the room directly at Damian and the sleazy alchemist before the latter takes off running. Damian, though, just stands there and takes the abuse — begging for her forgiveness as the wounds on his face re-open and bleed.

Half of his body was burned in the same fire he claims took Zai's life, but he's still alive, and she's... she's dead.

Dead.

"I—" I begin, trying to find my voice. "Someone needs to tell Mel. If I leave now, I can still catch—"

"No!" Mother roars.

I freeze in place, gritting my teeth.

"No," she repeats, stalking closer to Damian and grabbing a fistful of his hair. "No one leaves the city."

She drags Damian toward the back of the room, undoubtedly leading him to the dungeons, without another glance back at me.

Mother and I both know I will obey, even if I despise myself right now for it.

Still, I can't stay in this underground throne room of hers any longer. Before I know what I'm doing, I'm in the middle of the slums, staring up at a shabby building I last saw just hours ago.

I barely register sneaking inside and taking each despicable man out one by one, like the nightmare of their sins come back to haunt them.

A heartbeat passes, and I'm outside again.

The bottle in my hand is nearly empty now, all but a single drop of turpentine sloshed onto the wooden panels of the cramped house in front of me. A match rests in my trembling grasp, and my heartbeat is thundering so loudly in my ears, it almost drowns out my racing thoughts in the eerily quiet night.

Almost, but not quite.

My chest tightens and stomach twists as I think about my proud, fierce sister dying engulfed in flames.

I think about the despicable slavers inside, and the way they have brought nothing but misery to everyone around them.

Mostly, I think about the fact that Zaina might still be alive if I had gone after her instead of staying here, playing the good soldier to Mother and enabling men like the ones inside.

It's that last thought that finally propels me into motion. My fingers move automatically through the familiar action of dipping the match into a vial. A blue flame ignites at the end, flaring up to fill the glass before dying down to something smaller.

The flame dances down the brittle stick, closer and closer until it's nearly at my fingertips. Such a tiny thing to do so much damage.

To take a life.

With a flick of my wrist, I toss the match onto the wet doorway, and the flames burst and roar around me.

Fire burns around me, blazing in the window in blue and orange and yellow, surrounding my reflection like a macabre halo. I stare at the girl in the flames and empty obsidian eyes stare back at me, every inch of my heart-shaped face visible with my black hair pulled back into a braid.

I'm oddly relieved when the window shatters.

It isn't long before the fire engulfs everything. The house groans and the wooden furniture cracks and splits as the blaze climbs higher and higher, destroying everything in its path.

Tendrils of smoke find their way out and grasp for the stars, as if there is hope for an escape from the wreckage below.

But there isn't. Not for any of us.

Part of me knows I should leave. It's only a matter of time before people come to investigate, but I am mesmerized by the power of a single match. The shouts of the neighbors sound out, and I finally force myself back into the shadows.

The men inside that house will never wake up in time to escape their fate.

I search myself for some small semblance of guilt but come up empty. They will be unconscious when they die, a luxury my sister didn't have.

A luxury I won't have if Mother finds out about this.

Whatever she does will be slow. Merciless. Painful.

I have never defied her before. Out of loyalty or fear, I don't know anymore. I should be panicking.

Nevertheless, as the first shout of alarm goes up, and the flames creep threateningly on the ground near the alley, a quiet calm settles over me. I'm surrounded by smoke and fire and the lingering scent of death, but it feels as if I've taken my first real breath this evening.

That's when I decide these men will only be the first to go. There are two more vials in my bag and an endless sea of deserving targets for my particular brand of justice. Or vengeance.

If there's one thing Mother taught me, it's that you can never really separate the two.

CHAPTER TWO

ZAINA

TWO WEEKS LATER

J run my fingers along the edges of my crown, wondering at the power of such a delicate thing to change my life in a single night.

Just this morning, I was responsible only for myself and those I loved. Now, that responsibility extends to all of Jokith.

An unexpected wave of sadness fills me as I nestle the diadem into a velvet-lined box and shut it inside Einar's armoire.

I wore it for such a short time, but already, my head feels too light without the comforting weight, without the reminder of everyone who now falls under my protection and everything Einar and I stand to lose if we fail.

It's nearly time to go now.

Sigrid already came to say her final goodbye.

Or rather, to tell me that Jokithans do not give farewells, only promise to see one another later.

I pretended not to see the rare tears pooling in her eyes, and she pretended to believe me when I told her I would return. Perhaps she did believe me. If so, her faith is greater than my own.

Khijhana presses her enormous feline head against my legs, pulling me out of my thoughts just in time for me to steel my expression before Einar returns from his last walk of the castle.

His crown rests on his silvery-blond braids, adding just enough inches to his already substantial height that it nearly scrapes the top of the doorway when he enters.

"Everything is in place?" I ask him, searching his face for a sign that he's changed his mind about coming with me.

There is only resolve in his ice-blue eyes, though.

"It is. The messenger has been dispatched."

I nod, and a beat of silence passes.

"And you're sure you want to do this?" The question escapes my lips before I can catch it.

He examines my features, but I keep them neutral, not wanting to sway his decision. It's no small thing, leaving his people without their ruler for any amount of time. Let alone permanently.

"This plan is the best we've come up with," he finally says.

I don't miss the way he qualifies his statement. Not a good plan. The best out of several mediocre options. It's like juggling with the rusty knives instead of the freshly sharpened ones.

"Announcing my visit offers a layer of protection and gives us our best opportunity to sneak you in among the usual fanfare of a visiting monarch. Besides," he reminds me, "the king is an old friend. It would be an insult to enter his territory without informing him, and it's not as though Khijhana and I could remain unnoticed."

He raises a single eyebrow, and I suspect he intentionally did not answer the question the way I meant it.

Narrowing my eyes, I clarify. "I didn't mean the messenger."

"If you meant visiting Ulla, then I'm sure of that as well. We have nothing to lose by telling her the 'truth' of your death, since Dvain will have already told her about the dragon."

I don't quite flinch at the sound of the alchemist's name, but it's an effort.

I had almost forgotten that he was the one to deliver the news to Madame, one of the last things he did before I killed him.

He's dead, I remind myself. Gunnar and Helga burned his body so thoroughly that not a single bone shard remained.

It doesn't stop a thrum of panic from shooting through me, trailed by a tendril of unease every time I think about that day. Something doesn't feel quite right. It's like I'm playing a game of chess and haven't noticed the trap my opponent is setting.

Einar's mouth tightens, and I know he has noticed my reaction.

"Nothing to lose," I breathe. "What about your life? Don't think she can't find ways to kill you and make it look like an accident, whether the world knows you're visiting or not."

Einar crosses the white bear-skin rug to stand before me. Only when his warm hands land on my arms do I realize how cold I am. The hearth has long since gone out, the absence of the crackling fire making the space too still, too quiet.

"We knew the risks when we decided on this plan. Don't tell me my queen is backing out now."

The title still sounds strange on his lips.

"Of course not." I have no choice but to take on Madame. If she finds out I'm alive, she will come after me, my sisters, my husband, and likely all of Jokith.

And she will find out. The only question is when.

"We both know why we have to stop her, and we both know I couldn't sit here while you went alone any more than you could if the tables were turned." He pulls me closer, and I hesitate for only a moment before I allow myself to lean into him.

I doubt it will ever come easily to me, taking comfort from another person, but for his sake, I try. His sandal-wood scent envelops me, and I inhale deeply, soaking in the false sense of safety I feel in his arms before finally saying what I want to outright.

"I hate the idea of you having to be in the same room with her again. After everything she's done to you. After what she still might do."

"I hate it, too. But I don't see that we have any other options, since you seem fairly certain that hiring an assassin is out of the question." There's a grim smile in his voice. He's joking, and he isn't.

"If only. She's immune to every poison you can think of..." Something in the back of my mind snags on that, but I go on. "And she's strong, stronger than you could imagine. Whatever she's done to herself over the years, she's not quite human anymore." *If she ever was.*

We've been over this before, but the enormity of what

we're doing strikes me all over again as I say the words out loud.

That's not even what I'm the most worried about, and Einar must sense that.

"There's something else." It's not quite a question, but I surprise us both by answering anyway.

"Aika." Her name escapes my lips before I register thinking it.

"You're worried for her?"

For her. About her. I don't know how to explain to him the complexities of growing up with a monster, the way it can mold your mind in ways you can't possibly comprehend, ways you can't even see. The way it can trap your soul and turn you into someone you scarcely recognize.

Months spent away from Madame have hardly touched the hold she has on me, and Aika has never been away from her at all. Even on the island, she was steeped in every aspect of Madame's empire.

I don't want Einar to judge her, though, so I've avoided telling him this truth for too long. "I'm not sure we can count on her help," I finally say.

"Because you're worried about what will happen if she's caught in the crossfire? Or because she will be too afraid of the consequences?"

"If Aika is afraid of anything, she hides it well, even from me. What I mean is, I'm not sure she will be willing to go against Madame, because... she has a strong sense of loyalty, in her way." I search Einar's face for a hint of disdain, but he's only listening thoughtfully, so I go on. "Madame gave her a home, a family."

"Do you think we should go forward without her?" he asks uncertainly.

Leif knocks on the door to inform us that Gunnar and Helga are waiting for us at the carriage, and I use the break to consider what Einar asked.

Pulling the hood of my cloak down low, I let out a slow breath.

"I don't know that we *can* go forward without her. Regardless of whether we need her help, she's my sister. I'm not willing to go against her, and it would be nearly impossible to go around her. I just think it will need to be handled delicately." I shake my head, following Einar out the passageway door. "Honestly, I'm not even sure Aika knows what she stands for anymore."

CHAPTER THREE

AIKA

*I*t's been two weeks since my sister died.

That's the only excuse I have for letting the boy catch me off guard tonight.

Usually, I pride myself on vigilance... but I'm two drinks in and still buzzing with adrenaline from the fire I set only hours ago, and I have spent the evening steadfastly avoiding looking at the front door of the tavern.

Well, not the door, exactly. It's the empty barstool next to it, the one where Zaina used to sit, that I would just as soon never look at again.

It's bad enough that I can scarcely close my eyes without seeing my sister's perfect features and imagining the way they must have melted and twisted in the moments before the dragon took her.

At least here, I can escape all of that, losing myself in the drinks and the cards and the noise of the conversations around me.

I am raking in my winnings from the previous hand, putting on a show of triumph, when an irritatingly familiar voice startles me from across the table.

"Care for an actual challenge?"

Celestial Hells. Apparently, Zaina's ghost isn't the only one that wants to haunt me tonight.

It shouldn't be a surprise. The Drunken Pumpkin is close enough to King's Square that the guards come here often, and this guard in particular.

Hell, this is where I first met Remy.

Seeing him again should feel minor in the wake of my sister's death and a subsequent slew of arson, but this tavern is as close as I come to a sanctuary. The room I keep in town is just upstairs, and Remy hasn't come around nearly as often since our... whatever we had over a year ago.

"If only I knew where to find one." My mostly steady gaze drifts upward, scanning him from the black-and-crimson tunic that stretches across his broad chest to the unlikely dimple in his strong chin, the arrogant tilt to his full mouth.

Remy doesn't rise to my bait. He only tucks a wavy strand of chestnut hair behind his ear and sinks into the chair across from me like he owns it.

"Deal me in." Those were the first words I ever heard him say, back when he was just another mark and I was just a girl at the bar.

I down the rest of my cinnamon sake and signal for another before I speak again.

"Decide to crawl out of whatever hole you sank into and grace us with your presence?" Needling at him is the best distraction I've had all night.

"You sound sad." The serious undertone to his voice puts me on guard, but his expression is perfectly neutral as he surveys the five cards in his hands. "Did you miss me, Gemma?"

14

I don't bat an eye at the sound of the fake name.

Of my many monikers, that one, the one that represents the card shark and pickpocket, is the closest to feeling like my own.

"If I've been sad, it's only because no one was able to confirm your untimely demise." My voice falls flat on those last two words, too close to things I refuse to think about any more tonight. "And now this."

"By *this*, I assume you mean losing at your favorite game." He flashes me an expression that makes my toes curl, but I stamp down the feeling as quickly as it came.

"This is hardly my *favorite* game." My savage grin is more a baring of teeth, and I dare him to dance a little closer to all the things we never outright talk about. "And I wouldn't go right to losing."

My knuckle raps on the worn wooden table, the signal for another card, and Remy follows suit.

"No Lawrence tonight?" I ask after his hulking fellow guard, mostly to avoid an outward tell that the six of spades the dealer gave me was worthless to my hand.

I'll just have to bluff my way to a win.

"I'm sure he's around here somewhere." His tone is wry. "But your friend, Leila? She's still not back?"

Leila. It was the name Zai went by when she was here, and for a moment, I don't breathe. That's what I get for trying to misdirect him with idle chatter.

Hoping he doesn't notice my lapse, I will my features into neutrality.

"No." My tone is clipped, despite my best efforts. "She's not coming back."

There is no conversation after that, something my expression probably helps along. I order yet another cinnamon sake, hoping that it will help dull the pain that always accompanies thoughts of Zai.

The pile in the middle grows as Remy and I throw in coins of increasingly high value. I study his chiseled features, but they hold no clue as to whether he's bluffing the same as I am.

He returns my scrutiny. "You have to know when to fold, Gemma," he taunts.

I throw another silver on the pile in response, and he calls.

I lay out my pathetic hand with a flourish, hoping he's bluffing even worse than I am. But Remy tosses his head back and laughs, a full-bellied sound that mocks me before he splays out his royal flush.

"Bloody hell." I scowl.

I wouldn't be concerned about the loss if it were anyone else. The game is only part of why I come to the tavern. Primarily, I'm here for the same reason I do most things in my life.

Because Mother demands it.

This bar nestled near the mid-sector of town is the perfect place to gather information. Bits of gossip float to me, but all anyone wants to talk about tonight is *the vigilante*, which is what the newspapers have taken to calling me. Not that they know I'm the one setting the fires.

So I let the voices fade into the background, effectively tuning them out...all except for the high pitched giggle of the barmaid when she "accidentally" falls into Remy's lap for the seventh time, something he is actively encouraging.

"Some things never change," I mutter, grateful for the distraction from my darker thoughts. "At least you'll make this one an easy win for me."

That's not strictly true, when he is giving no discernible tells.

"Don't worry your pretty little head about that. I'm an excellent multi-tasker, or don't you remember?" He's had several ales himself, and he practically purrs the words.

"I *do* remember. Multitasking with me and half the town, it seemed," I reply in an even tone. Not that I can judge him, much, but at least I waited until we ended things to return to my usual parade of unsuspecting marks.

He arches a dark brown eyebrow. "Are you sure about that, Gemma? I'm surprised you can *commit* yourself to that accusation."

I let out a soft snort. Like the man would have been able to commit himself to anything besides his next drink.

Remy has bet his entire pile of coins by the time I call. He shows his hand first with a confident grin on his perfectly shaped lips.

I can't help but taunt him a little in return, twirling each card between my fingers with a flourish before revealing them one at a time.

Remy's grin falters a bit with each card, fading entirely when I slowly overturn my last one.

I force my lips up in a show of triumph, though it's as hollow as the rest of me feels.

Remy groans. "One more round?" he offers.

"And give you a chance to redeem yourself?" I slide my winnings into my coin purse, securing it to my belt before getting to my feet. "I think I'll pass."

"Redeem myself?" he scoffs. "I won as many as you did."

"But I won the last one," I remind him. "And you know only the most recent win counts."

It's a tired argument, but almost comforting in its familiarity. Or it would be, with someone less aggravating.

"Won't you at least buy me a consolation drink, then?" Remy stands as well, moving around the table and edging in close to me. Too close, but I'll be damned if I give him the satisfaction of moving away.

"Tempting as it is, that's a road I'd just as soon never travel again." Just one of many lies I've told tonight, but this one, by all rights, should be the truth.

He opens his mouth to respond when the bartender slides a chilled glass with a copper-colored liquid in front of me. "Someone ordered a Widow's Kiss for the victor."

I sigh. Three cherries garnish the top, a sign that Mother needs me urgently. I'm torn between feeling grateful for the excuse to leave and frustrated that Remy will think I'm running away, but in the end, I lack the conviction to feel either for very long.

I take the toothpick with the black, liqueur-soaked cherries from the glass and slide them off with my teeth before passing the rest to Remy.

"Looks like you got that drink after all. I'll see you around." With that, I grab the coin purse from the counter and stride out into the biting night air.

Zai's death has made Mother more volatile than usual. If she has summoned me to come quickly, even I am not brave enough to keep her waiting tonight.

CHAPTER FOUR
AIKA

$\mathcal{T}$he streets are nearly empty at this hour, shadows punctuated by the silvery light of the full moon. The darkness is welcome, but my thoughts sound unnaturally loud in the silence, relentlessly echoing in my head.

It's almost a relief when Remy's familiar measured footsteps pad against the cobblestone road behind me. I don't slow my pace, though, because he doesn't need to know that.

"When I said I would see you around, I didn't mean right now." My words are punctuated with white puffs of air that dissolve into the shadows as quickly as they come.

I wish I could disappear as easily, if only to avoid whatever has Mother calling me back at nearly midnight.

"I just thought our friend back there might miss the coins you swiped off of him." Remy's long strides easily overtake me.

"Then he should guard them more carefully." I shrug, not remotely sorry to steal from a man who spends more money on his mistress than his wife.

A dry laugh escapes Remy's lips, and I hate how the sound makes the air around us feel several degrees warmer.

Bastard.

"Don't you make enough money hustling cards that you don't need to steal?" He nudges me with his arm.

"Of course I do, but where would be the fun in that?" I say, pushing him away.

"How very upstanding of you. It's a wonder we didn't work out."

"Indeed, especially given the endless stream of other women who were always coming to fetch you from the tavern in the wee hours of the night."

That's only partly true. What came between us was that I had pledged my loyalty to Mother long before Remy came along, and relationships that don't benefit her are not in the cards for me.

Which is fine, really. I wouldn't know what to do with a real relationship, anyway.

"I'm surprised you're still holding onto that, considering you spend more nights away from your room than in it." He gestures vaguely to the room above the tavern that I'm clearly walking away from.

"And I'm surprised you notice anything that isn't falling into your lap, but here we are." Realizing that my comment sounds nearly as jealous as his did, I turn to leave before he can press the issue.

He's at my heels within seconds.

"I'm not giving you the purse back," I huff, winding my way through the alleys closer to the mid-sector.

I don't need the man's gold, but there's an orphanage around the corner that most certainly does.

"Oh, that old bastard's coins?" He snorts. "I wouldn't

dream of asking for those back. But I wouldn't be a gentleman if I didn't escort a lady walking so late at night, on your way to... where did you say you were going?"

I roll my eyes at his blatant fishing, and the idea that anything on these streets would be more dangerous than I am.

"I see no gentlemen here." I spread my arms to indicate the lack.

Remy's hand goes to his heart as if I've physically wounded him.

"I could pretend to be one for tonight. Now, where are we going?" he tries again.

"Don't ask questions you don't want the answer to."

He pulls my arm gently until I stop, finally turning to look at him. His cinnamon eyes bore into mine with an intimacy that brings back memories and feelings better left buried.

"And what about questions I do want the answer to?" His voice is soft as he leans down, his face inches from my own.

I despise the way the air crackles between us, the way he tugs at something in me that has been firmly shut off in the two weeks since my sister died. I despise everything about this moment until he... takes a deep whiff of my hair.

My brow furrows.

"For example," he asks. "Why do you smell like smoke?"

A fraction of a heartbeat is all I hesitate. It's hardly any time at all, but more of a tell than I ever give. I scramble to recover, doing what I do best.

I lie.

"A *friend* of mine quite enjoys it. I was with him before

21

I came here, and since you insisted on asking, that's where I'm headed now."

The best lies play on the emotions of the person, and I'm banking on stirring up enough jealousy or at least intrigue to cover my slip.

But his careful features reveal nothing when he dips closer to me.

My heart beats a little faster in my chest, and I can't tell if it's because of his proximity or if I actually have the sense to be afraid. Not of him, but of what it might mean for me if word gets out that I'm the vigilante.

He narrows his eyes, inches from mine. "So you wouldn't know anything about the recent string of fires, then?"

I force out a disbelieving laugh "Rest assured, Remy. If I were going to randomly set people on fire, I would have started with you." My fingers press against his solid chest until he backs away.

I fold my arms over my corseted bodice, suddenly colder than the temperature accounts for.

"Obviously, I don't think you incapacitated several grown men and then burned them alive, Gemma." He shakes his head like the mere notion is absurd. "But you always have your ear to the ground, and I have a suspicion you might know something... might have even seen something."

I almost wish I could tell him I *had* done it just to wipe that patronizing look off his face.

"Well, I don't, and I didn't."

The enormous bell at Palais Etienne chimes the first of its midnight tolls, reminding me that I have allowed myself to linger too long.

We are at the edge of the Heights, the wealthiest part

of town. Bright paper lanterns line the road here, so at least he has no excuse to follow me when I turn to leave again.

"Trust me, Remy. No one knows anything about who the vigilante really is."

It might be the truest thing I've said all night.

CHAPTER FIVE
AIKA

The rest of my trek home is eventless. I make a small detour to drop the coin purse at the orphanage, leaving it in the usual spot behind a garbage bin, then take the quickest route back to Mother's.

I head through the back gate because it's the fastest path to the mausoleum Mother had built for her fictitious dead husband, my "father."

The lanterns around the crypt are lit, a sign that she is conducting business. The usual guards are stationed outside, but they are for little more than show — cannon fodder if someone actually decides to attack her.

Mother is her own line of defense.

Nodding to the stoic guards, I go through the small door at the back of the stone building, bypassing the empty tomb and heading straight for a door that looks like it should lead to a closet.

Instead, cramped stairs wind downward, each flight an odd number of steps. It's a pattern I know by heart, ending at the narrow walkway deep underground that I am intimately familiar with.

No matter how many times I've walked this hall, I never feel any less uneasy about it. The salty sea air can't mask the residue of death and suffering that coats the very walls of this place.

Which is fitting, considering the woman who owns it.

The hallway comes to an end at Mother's makeshift throne room. Only the faint glow of the eerie purple lanterns lights up the cave-like room, enhancing the darkness rather than illuminating it.

Elegant curtains line the walls, covering the windows that have been carved into the cliff face so she can look out over the sea whenever she wants to. It's the single feature all of her dwellings have in common.

Well, that and the dungeons.

Tonight, though, the curtains are closed, not allowing so much as a stray beam of moonlight to enter.

I am vaguely surprised to find that Mother is not lounging in her regal chair as usual, but that feeling dissipates when I see what she's doing instead. She stands near the gilded chair, dangling a full-grown man off the ground with a single hand wrapped tightly around his neck.

The man bucks and scratches at her arms, but his fingernails don't penetrate. I've never seen anything successfully scratch her skin, not that many have been stupid enough to try.

"You sent for me, Mother?" I use the title she has insisted upon since we met.

Mother's long lashes slant downward as she slides her violet gaze over to me. She is the picture of calm, not so much as twitching her eyebrow when the man's boot connects solidly with her shin.

Eventually, his kicks weaken, and his protests ebb

away. Only when he has been still for several moments does she let his body drop, responding to me.

"Yes, my child." Her voice is calm, not a shred of inflection to betray what she's feeling. "There was another fire tonight."

My mouth goes dry, my mind racing.

If she knew I was the one setting the fires, I would surely be in the dungeons by now. *Or dead, if she's feeling merciful.*

"So I heard." I don't bother to act surprised since she'll see through any attempt. "I went to the scene in case there were survivors to question, but there were none."

Lie. But at least that will account for the lingering smell of smoke clinging stubbornly to my dress.

Her eyes narrow before she nods.

"It was one of our newly acquired establishments, one you visited earlier this week." It's not a question, but I respond anyway.

"Fires, when your primary enforcer is known as The Flame. Do you think whoever is doing this is mocking us?" I inject a bit of offense into my tone.

"If they are, they will not be doing so for long." Her voice is like a thousand shards of jagged ice, the threat lingering in the air as though she's willing it into reality. "Paolo, here, was watching the building in question, since this *vigilante* has gone after every other slaver in the city, and yet, he managed to see nothing."

She looks disdainfully at the corpse. I glance down at his face again and recognize him as the man she assigned to investigate the fires. *My fires.*

There is a slight tug in the back of my mind that recognizes that his death is my fault, but I shrug it off. No

27

one in Madame's organization is innocent. We all deserve whatever end we meet.

A shadow moves in the pitch-black corner behind her. My hand goes automatically to one of my false pockets, pulling out the throwing stars strapped to my thigh. The figure steps close enough for me to recognize, and my lip curls in disgust.

"*Brother.* I see you're back from your holiday." Reluctantly, I return my weapons to their holster.

I'm not in any danger from him here. Mother may have let him out of the dungeons, but she clearly hasn't forgiven him even enough to heal the oozing wounds on his face, let alone for him to hurt her last reliable *asset.*

Damian doesn't flinch at the reminder of his time in Mother's tender care, and I'd be lying if I said I wasn't disappointed by his lack of reaction.

Mother turns her stare on me, so like her only biological daughter's. But where Mel is pure kindness and light, Mother's eyes are empty. I have seen more than my share of death, have watched the light and life bleed from someone's face until their body is little more than an empty husk.

Mother's eyes are even emptier than that, an endless abyss where no sound or life or light dares to penetrate.

"This has to end, before every halfwit in the city believes they can undermine my operation," she says evenly.

"Would you like me to investigate them before I go back to Delphine?" I ask in an effort to cover for myself, as well as see when she plans to send me back to the Chateau.

The seas around Delphine aren't traversable in the

winter months. If I stay in Bondé much longer, I'll be stuck here until the spring.

"Damian." Mother gestures vaguely toward the body, and Damian rushes to do her bidding, pulling the body out of the room.

All the while, my heart beats an unsteady staccato in my ears, reminding me that Zaina was not the first of Madame's *daughters* who was sacrificed for her cause.

I was chosen as a replacement for Rose, and it is in my best interest, always, to remain useful to Mother.

Lest she find a replacement for me.

"*D*amian is being allowed a chance to redeem himself." Mother shatters the silence. "He will be investigating the fires from now on."

If I didn't already feel so hollow, I would now.

Not only am I not going back to Melodi at the Chateau on the island, but now Damian will be investigating me. He might be a monster, but he's not a fool. Besides, he would love nothing more than to see me fall.

She didn't order him away just to tell me that, though.

Mother crosses the small distance between us, her heels clacking on the stone. Approaching me, she reaches out her hand to cup my cheek. Her touch is ice and death, but I can't help the small part of me that leans into it.

She's the only mother I've ever known, after all.

"An opportunity has arisen for us, *daughter*." She moves her hand to trace an old scar in my brow. "You'll have to be more careful now, Aika. No more work that could damage your hands or face. I need you looking pristine."

I go still. It will be impossible to do my job as her enforcer and be careful, but that never mattered before.

On the rare occasions I need to be Lady Aika Delmara, I wear gloves over my scarred knuckles and heavy cosmetics on my face.

So why now?

"Am I going somewhere?" I ask carefully.

"I have finally convinced the *hag* to bring her son out of hiding."

She makes her way to the window, throwing open the black velvet curtains to allow the light of the moon to brighten the room around us.

"Honestly, if I had known she was going to turn into a hermit, I would have let the older one live a little longer," she mutters. Then, in a louder voice, "The queen is throwing Corentin's traditional masquerade ball for her remaining son, and unlike his brother, he *will* choose his bride from the ladies presented there."

A thousand thoughts run through my mind. The royal family sequestered their remaining children after the heir died under "mysterious" circumstances, along with the commoner he had just eloped with. This news will rock all of Corentin, with every last noble throwing their daughters at Prince Francis in an effort to climb higher in rank.

But for Mother to bring this up means...

"You want me to marry the prince," I say without inflection.

Mother turns back to me, pride shining in her expression.

"Exactly. All you will need to do is be present and make a show of spending time with the prince. I've already handled the rest." She looks me over intently. "At least it is a *masquerade ball*."

Indeed.

"Oh, and, Aika?" Something in her voice makes me steel myself for another twist of the knife. "You will need to stay here more often than you have been. We have an image to maintain now that you will be more obvious in society."

"Of course." My lips have gone numb.

The limited freedom I have managed to wrangle is being ripped away from me, piece by piece. Before I can think better of it, I find myself asking another question.

"What is my objective?" I wait for her to bestow the same life sentence she did on Zaina. The bearing of an heir.

Mother arches a perfectly manicured brow and stares at me for a long moment before answering.

"I need a specific piece of information, something only imparted to the royal family. I'm sure with your skills, it won't take you long to obtain it."

I let out a subtle sigh of relief. Short term, then, and no babies required. I open my mouth to ask what information, but she silences me with a raised hand.

"That's all you need to know for now." She waves her hand toward the door, signaling the end of our conversation.

I stride from the room without hesitation, reminding myself with each step how much worse this could be.

At least I'll never go hungry there. Though it's been years since I was starving on the streets, that gnawing feeling in my belly never feels quite far enough from me.

By the time I reach my rooms, I've almost managed to convince myself this will be a good thing.

I bolt awake after only four short hours of sleep, my neck and back covered in a sheen of sweat, but then, that's hardly newsworthy. I've long since grown used to the nightmares that haunt me, the only things in my life that have never abandoned me.

Besides Mother, of course.

It takes a moment to orient myself in the vast room of the estate, so unlike the cramped one I rent above The Drunken Pumpkin. This one is pristine, all rich colors and plush fabrics. The bed could fit six of me, and the fur-lined blankets are warmer than anything I keep in my room above the tavern.

That room still feels more fitting for a girl like me, rickety bed and all. Twelve years later, and the opulence of this entire estate still feels like someone else's life.

Then again, sometimes the bloodshed feels that way too.

I pull a simple gray dress from my wardrobe, one that won't stand out too much in the slums. My enforcer's mask is carefully concealed in the back of the dresser, where it will stay for the foreseeable future. Pure white lacquer with a single blue flame under the left eye for the identity Madame made me.

The Flame. Her Flame.

Until now.

Now, she's molding me into something else entirely.

🔥

It's a long walk from the estate to the slums, but I don't mind.

The exertion helps me drown out the thoughts running on a loop through my head, and it's easy to lose myself in the mass of people crowding the streets.

Bondé is a port city, a melting pot of every known culture and a few that aren't, so the faces that pass me range from deep onyx to translucently pale, with every shade in between. The perfect place to blend in.

My first stop is to see if the vendors have any information for me. Specifically, the baker, today.

When I catch his eye, he gives me a subtle shake of his head.

Since he has nothing for me, I dig in my purse for a small coin instead of the silver I had out for him, tossing it over. In return, he hands me a basket made from newspapers, full of sugar crusted puffs of dough and a sweet berry dipping sauce.

As I walk down the street, I inhale the heady scent of the food, my mouth watering before I can pull out my chopsticks to take my first bite. Dipping one of them into the sauce, I pop it into my mouth and groan with pleasure. The berries and crusted sugar explode across my tongue, and my eyes roll to the back of my head in response.

I'm just lifting the second one to my lips when a familiar chuckle reaches me from the shadows.

"Really, Gemma, a whole basket? Someone's in a mood today."

An irritable sigh escapes me.

"Stalking now, Remy? I would say that's low, even for you, but it wouldn't quite be true, given your day job," I say bitterly, taking my next bite.

"Says the thief?" His eyes spark with genuine offense.

"At least I don't parade around pretending to be doing something noble." I gesture to his pristine uniform, evidence that he hasn't set foot in the dirty alleys of the slums today where most of the actual crime happens.

"At least I try to reduce the crime in this city instead of adding to it," he bites back.

"That kind of moral high ground really only works for people who don't actually have to live in the reality of the world they *aren't* improving." I sigh, losing whatever energy I had for an ethical debate as quickly as it came.

He takes in my expression, his own softening. I scowl, but he just reaches for one of the fried balls of dough in my basket.

So, I stab his hand with the pointier end of my chopstick.

"Ow." He pulls back dramatically. "You just make thieving sound so appealing, I thought I'd give it a try."

I roll my eyes. "I think it's safe to say pick-pocketing is not among your repertoire of skills. You're lucky I didn't go for my dagger."

"I should have remembered you don't like to share your food, I suppose."

"Altruism really isn't my strong suit," I say, shoving another bite into my mouth.

"Then why do you leave money for the orphanage?" He raises his eyebrows, a bit of genuine curiosity peeking through.

I knew I hadn't lost him quickly enough last night. Hopefully he was the only one who noticed. Being charitable is a weakness that others can use against you, but giving to the orphanage isn't something I'm willing to give up.

I'll just have to be more cautious going forward.

"I wasn't," I lie, and it's not even a good one.

"Careful, Gemma." He leans forward, his tone a blend of seriousness and teasing that he has perfected. "Your mask is slipping."

"Did you need something?" I shove him away, deliberately changing the subject. "Or did you have nothing better to do than track me down for the purpose of irritating me today?"

"I'm so glad you asked. I could use your help." His eyes focus on something behind me toward King's Square, and I turn to see Lawrence striding down the walkway. The man's ebony face is like a thundercloud, and Remy holds up a hand to stave him off.

"Why would I help you do anything?" I turn back to Remy.

He hesitates for a second before answering. "For old time's sake?"

"Old time's sake would have me stabbing you through the eye." I have every intention of dismissing him outright, but curiosity gets the better of me. "But just for fun, let's say I'm willing to help. What do you want?"

"I need information on the vigilante. Or better yet, on a woman named Madame."

I choke back a laugh, barely. *Of course he does.*

"And I need a diamond-encrusted blade resting upon a mountain of freshly steamed pork buns, but we can't all have what we want, now can we?"

Remy throws his head back in a full-bellied laugh, and it seeps through to every part of me. I turn to leave, but his voice follows in my wake.

"Indeed. For instance, I'm sure you don't *want* me to go to the magistrate with my information on the vigilante."

I freeze, my heart dropping into my stomach. "You don't have any information on the vigilante."

"A mysterious girl who smells like woodsmoke? It will be your word against mine, and he's an old friend." His words are casual enough that I almost believe him, but then, bluffing is what Remy does best.

I rotate slowly to face him, pretending that his words don't make me feel like I'm balancing on the balcony of the Chateau, one strong gale away from being dashed against the jagged rocks below.

"You would falsely accuse me? What about all your precious moral high ground?" My voice is lower than before, careful of any listening ears in the crowd around us.

"I seem to recall you telling me that was for people who didn't have to live in reality. You should be happy that I've decided to lower myself to your level." He matches my volume this time.

I had said that and meant it, but I never expected it to come back and haunt me this way.

"Don't you have enough to do without chasing ghosts?" I try a different tactic.

"The vigilante is hardly a ghost, and I'd venture to say Madame is real enough, judging by the look on your face when I mentioned her."

My stomach hollows, and it's an effort to keep my features neutral. Remy has caught me off guard twice now in as many days. I choose my words carefully, trying to answer the way an actual low-level pickpocket would.

"No one with any sense has heard of Madame." I allow a bit of fear to enter my gaze. "If you were smart, you'd forget you had either."

"Would that I could." His deep brown eyes meet mine, his hand going almost subconsciously to the sword belted at the waist of his uniform. "Especially since all I seem to be getting are answers like yours. Even my infallible charm hasn't been enough to convince anyone to talk, except for a handful of vague hints from people who have since disappeared under *questionable* circumstances."

"Seems like a solid reason to let it go."

He arches a brow. "But it's my job to lower crime, and she seems to be intent on raising it."

"Don't kid yourself, Remy. The criminals in this city have existed long before her and will keep on long after she's gone." Not that I think she'll ever really be gone.

Still, it's true enough. Mother might profit from the crime, but she only organizes what was already there.

"Ah, but they're bolder now. And whoever this vigilante is, he clearly isn't afraid of her."

He. It's an effort not to scoff.

"So, people are being killed for just thinking about talking and you feel like it's a good idea to keep pushing?" I hope my expression conveys exactly how stupid I think he is.

Especially since I've helped create the dead end he's

running into, and I don't particularly want him up next on my list of people to frighten into submission. My worlds are coming perilously close to colliding.

Remy and I wouldn't be the only casualties in that disaster.

"Well, what can I say? I've got nothing better to do." The stubborn tilt of his chin is at odds with his nonchalant tone, but both tell me I'm going to get nowhere convincing him to leave this alone.

But I'm also not going to help him commit suicide.

"That's admirable, truly. I'll put it on your tombstone. Sadly, you might not have qualms about risking your life, but I have no desire to risk mine." Speaking of which, I throw a surreptitious glance around to make sure no one is looking at me with too much interest.

I'd rather not explain this encounter to Mother later. Time to wrap this up.

"I'm going to have to decline. You should get back to Lawrence, anyway. He's looking even more uptight than usual."

This is not untrue, as Lawrence paces irritably and gestures to his pocket watch.

Remy ignores his friend, his lips parting in disbelief. "You would rather be accused of burning people alive than help me? At this point, there's no guarantee of a fair trial. They would hang a dozen men and women if it meant one of them might be the vigilante. You'll get the noose if you're convicted."

I resist the urge to swallow back a wave of bile. Mother rewards those who are loyal to her, but if she finds out I have betrayed her by helping him, I'll be begging for the noose.

Less than a second passes while I weigh my options,

each choice like a leaky boat in a churning sea. So I pick the one I believe will hold up the longest, calling Remy on what I sincerely hope is one of his many bluffs.

"I'll take my chances with the hangman." I shrug, turning to leave. "At least that would be a quick death."

CHAPTER EIGHT

AIKA

*A*fter my annoying encounter with Remy, I head deeper into the slums to see if any of the street urchins have any news. They make the perfect spies, since no one looks twice at an orphan.

Except for Mother, anyway. She saw me even when I was trying not to be seen

"You're different from the others." The strangely beautiful woman puts her hand on my chin, turning my face toward her. "How would you like to come live with me?"

"I'm not a brothel girl." I hurriedly take several steps back, and the woman's face softens into a semblance of a smile, though there is still no warmth in it.

"I'm not speaking of anything so crass as that, my girl. Just things like this, like you're already doing, but instead they would be at my discretion. In return, you'll have a roof over your head, food in your belly. Best of all, you'll have a family."

I'm no one's fool.

There is darkness in this woman behind her perfectly mani- cured fingernails and coiffed hair and the smile that doesn't

quite reach her eyes. But I'm also hungry, and tired, and what she's proposing sounds better than the life I'm living now.

My hesitation is all the encouragement she needs to extend her hand to me, and the answering growl of my stomach is enough to make me take it.

I didn't realize then that her offer was permanent, that the only way out of it was death.

A girl slinks up to me, pulling me from the memory.

"Jessa." I ruffle a hand through her lice-ridden hair, and she pretends to hate it. "Do you have anything for me?"

"Do *you* have anything for *me*?" she demands.

I've taught her well.

Jessa bears little resemblance to me. Her angular eyes are blue, and her hair is a tangled mass of light-brown curls, but something in her dirty face and sly, determined expression has always reminded me of myself .

Maybe it's the hollow cheekbones and jutting collarbone that make me pay her for the things she hears, along with a handful of others.

Or maybe it's that, for all I tell myself I'm better off with Mother having found me, I don't want them to have to make the same choices I did.

Whatever it is, I hand over a couple of coins and the rest of my fried dough. She pockets the coppers and tears into the bread with her teeth, talking around the mouthful.

"More kids are disappearing."

"Going to work on the ships?" I ask. That isn't unusual in the slums closest to the harbor.

She gives me a look like I'm an idiot. "No. Stolen. Younger than the ones as work for the shippers."

I bite back a curse.

"Slavers." The bastards are getting bolder, now that Madame has taken them under her protection. Every time I burn one group to the ground, two more pop up in its place.

Still, it's satisfying enough work. Looks like someone just got moved to the top of my list.

Jessa's expression is fierce, but her small form is frail. Some long-forgotten instinct has me warning her.

"Remember to only report what you hear freely. Don't put yourself in danger. And for stars' sake, if the slavers are out in full force, don't go out after dark."

"That's the best time for nicking!" she protests.

I toss another coin her way. "There. Now you won't have to."

She only gives me a dubious look.

"Anything else?" I hold out another copper, closing my fist when she reaches for it.

She scowls, but answers. "That Jokith King, he's on his way here."

"What?" My tone is sharper than I intended. "How do you know that?" Usually, she only knows what's going on in the city.

"One of the palace runners has a brother 'round here."

I toss her the copper, my mind racing. The king hasn't left Jokith in at least a decade. The borders are shut down so tight it took me weeks just to find Zai, let alone get a letter through.

Though he got his false story about my sister's untimely fall from a horse out just fine.

Is he coming to admit what a liar he is? To pretend to grieve a woman he publicly dubbed his plaything and knew a whole three months?

For all the numbness I have felt lately, the news about

the king makes my blood thunder in my veins. Whatever his reasons for coming, it's a chance for me to get some answers.

*T*here is no air.

Logically, I know that isn't true, know that this trunk has been specifically modified to provide more than enough air for the short bursts of time I stay in here.

My mind knows that, but my body remembers being trapped in a different trunk. It remembers being eclipsed by frigid water and ice until my lungs caught fire.

My body remembers death, or however close to it I came in those interminable moments in the cave.

By the time Einar lifts the wooden lid off the trunk, I have arranged my features into a semblance of calm. But he is not fooled.

"I hate this," he mutters darkly, his pale blue eyes searing into mine.

"At least we know the extra guards on the border are doing their jobs." *Even if their thoroughness did have me in the trunk for twice as long as I expected to be.* I try for a lighter tone than I feel, maneuvering myself onto the carriage bench next to him.

Which is easier said than done, since Khijhana lounges

on the floor, taking up nearly all the room that my trunk doesn't, and casts irritable glances at us every time we hit a bump.

Not that I blame her. The first carriage we rode in had slats instead of wheels, gliding smoothly along the snow, but we switched it out for a traditional style when the snow began to lessen toward the Corentine border.

I missed it as soon as it was gone.

The carriage. The snow. Jokith.

"True," Einar responds to my statement about the guards. "I told you the resources of a king are good for something."

A shaft of light creeps through the drawn velvet curtains, illuminating Einar's uptilted lips, but there's an undercurrent to his words, a wound that will take more than a handful of weeks to heal.

If I had trusted in his resources, we wouldn't be in the position we are now. If I had trusted in *him*.

He slides closer to me, slowly, giving me a chance to pull away. I wish I could say it wasn't necessary, but my body needs time to remember that I am safe here after Dvain put his disgusting hands on me only four days ago.

I close the distance between us, and Einar stretches an arm around me, suffusing me with his endless well of warmth. It penetrates my fur-lined cloak, seeping against my skin, until I feel like I can breathe again.

Being pulled back to the day I was taken, the day Odger stuffed me in that trunk, has made me realize what's been nagging at me about the alchemist. Besides the usual unending revulsion.

"How did Dvain know about the dragon?" I ask out loud.

Einar told me that his former ambassador brought up

the dragon, that it was part of how he revealed himself to be a traitor and a liar. *But how did he know?*

Einar glances down at me, his brow furrowed.

"I assumed from whoever was watching you and *Damian*." He spits the name out with nearly as much abhorrence as I feel.

I consider that. Madame always has one person to watch another. My entire plan that day when I went to the dragon hinged on that very idea, but...

"Why go north to report to the alchemist?"

Einar chews his lip, mulling that over. "Ulla instructed him to report to Dvain first?"

"Maybe." My agreement is dubious.

There isn't a better explanation, but I still can't shake the feeling that I'm missing something.

Something important. Something that should be obvious, except that every time I try to think about the night in the cave or at the alchemist's, my mind careens into a different direction.

I press my fingers against my temples in frustration. Einar's hands gently cover mine, lowering them from my face. His right thumb traces the lines of my moonstone ring, and warmth spreads through me.

His lips are close to mine and I want to move closer to them, to lose myself in them entirely, but I cast around for a reason I shouldn't.

"We need to talk about—"

"Literally nothing that we haven't already discussed to death. Helga and Gunnar have our security taken care of, and there's nothing else we can plan right now." He doesn't move closer, though, and I know he understands the real reason I am stalling.

I know, too, that he will accept without offense or

judgment if I back away from him, if I move to the other side of the carriage.

That knowledge emboldens me to move ever so slightly forward.

"Perhaps it is time for a break," I allow, my mouth so close to his that our breaths converge into a single misty cloud.

The sight tugs at something low in my belly, and still, he doesn't move. Finally, I give into myself, erasing the remaining space between us.

Whatever heat I felt from him a moment ago explodes into something else entirely when my mouth meets his, when my tongue darts out to taste him. For all that I have struggled to escape the maddening rote of the thoughts and plans marching through my mind, every single one of them dissipates in this moment.

All I know, all I feel, is Einar.

His hand goes to my waist, pulling me even tighter against him, and the other tangles in my midnight hair.

I drink in the feel of his skin against mine, losing myself in the way I can almost believe that this tiny bubble of reality is all there is, that there is no Madame and no nightmares and no inevitable death waiting on the horizon.

I can almost believe we might be free of her one day.

CHAPTER TEN
AIKA

*M*other is *occupied* with one of the poor bastards who works for her when I return home, so I take the coward's way out and slip a note under the door. I suspect she won't take the news of the arrival of the Jokithan King's arrival well.

Then I head to the rooms underneath the mausoleum to find Damian.

Too many questions still surround Zaina's death, and his tale is so at odds with the version the king told. I can't shake the feeling that there is more to Damian's story, regardless of what he told Mother.

I don't bother knocking before letting myself into his room.

"Did you want something, street rat?" he asks from his seat by the fire.

Unwanted and cast off as he was, Damian is the son of a lord, something he never lets me forget.

"Indeed, I do, *bastard*." My insult lands more solidly than his did.

His mangled features tighten in response, though he covers it quickly.

Moving over to the chair adjacent to his, I sit on the arm, with all of the casualness of someone who feels at home, even though being in Damian's room or in his presence is the equivalent to swimming in the sewers with my mouth open.

"I have a few questions for you, ones I would have asked sooner, but I know that you were *tied up* for a while. How does it feel to be out of the dungeons and back in the crypt, where you belong?" I bat my eyes in mock innocence. "Don't you just love how Mother keeps you out here, away from the rest of the household. You know... like a dog?"

Damian stares at me, his cold, dead eyes giving nothing away, until the corner of his mouth lifts slightly.

"Oh, Aika." He says my name condescendingly, pouring two glasses from a decanter of spirits. "How does it feel to know that *you* will never truly be a part of her family? That you'll never be anything more than the dirty orphan Mother brought home one day to replace the daughter she actually wanted. If someone here is the stray, it isn't me."

I take the proffered glass before he notices my clenched fists, hating that he's turned the tables on me. Hating even more that I have no rebuttal for his words.

"And what makes you think that you are any different?"

Damian chuckles, a dry, humorless sound. "Once I prove my loyalty, she has promised to give Melodi to me. Then, I will be her son, in truth." His expression unnerves me, but I keep my features neutral.

On the inside, my stomach drops and I'm not nearly as

calm as I appear to be. I barely resist the urge to shatter the glass against his skull and grind the shards into his ruined flesh for daring to imagine that he could touch Mel, let alone marry her.

The hell he will.

His dark eyes follow my every move, waiting for me to call him on his bluff, or rather, waiting for me to challenge the truth of his words.

Damian's lip twists in a disturbed grin, like he hears every dark thought that races through my head.

"Bold of you to assume she'll keep that promise." I grit my teeth, crooning the words. "Especially when she doesn't publicly claim you."

"*Mother* is not the liar in this family." His tone is as bored as ever, but the way he emphasizes that puts me on edge.

I wait until he takes a sip of his drink before sniffing my own glass.

It's a smoked whiskey, woodsy and sooty, but there is a trace of something else there, too. Something sweet.

Hul gil. Liquid poppies.

Not terribly original for a man who claims to be the son of an alchemist, but I doubt he was trying to kill me. More likely, he wanted to put me in a compromising position, something to make me look bad.

"Speaking of liars... Tell me again why Zaina insisted on going with you to that cave?"

Damian's eyes dart up to meet mine.

"Come now, Damian. You wouldn't want me to tell Mother that you were being... difficult, would you?"

His jaw twitches before he responds, no trace of amusement left in his tone. "She didn't trust me to get the job done."

"Well, that was certainly fair, considering what happened. So, then you... what? Just wandered into a cave that happened to have a dragon in it?" I leave my chair to walk closer to him, propping one leg up on the arm of his seat, my hand playing with the hilt of my dagger. "I think you're lying. I think that you killed her."

I stare into his eyes far longer than I would like, waiting for the second he admits it so I can finally kill him.

Damian laughs the same mirthless sound as before.

"And then what? I set myself on fire?" He gestures to the still-healing burns on his face and neck. "As usual, you've managed to miss the mark. I would never betray Mother that way."

Liar. Rising from the arm of the chair, I take a step back, securing both of my feet on the floor.

"Yes, you would. You would betray anyone if you thought there would be no repercussions for it. You're a sociopath, Damian. A lying, murdering, soulless sociopath."

I toss the liquid in my glass at him. His face takes on a murderous expression as he quickly tries to wipe it off, unconcerned with the cloth tearing at his ruined flesh. He growls at me, spitting out the drops that made it into his mouth.

"Enjoy that dose of *hul gil* you tried to share with me." I spin around, calling over my shoulder, "I certainly hope it wasn't the lethal kind."

CHAPTER ELEVEN

AIKA

*I*t's another fitful night of sleep, haunted by Damian's words and Jessa's news and Remy's troubling questions, and most of all, by the unshakable feeling that I finally see what I've been missing about Zaina's death.

Pushing the thoughts from my head, I make my way to King's Square with my fiddle case. The city is already beginning to stir by the time I get there.

The bells above the shopkeepers' doors and the clacking of vendors rolling their carts into place play out like a melody designed to accompany my instrument.

Plopping down in my usual spot, I ready my fiddle to play. This process of tightening the bow and adding rosin used to soothe me. In another life, perhaps I could have simply enjoyed playing just for the music, rather than using it as a ruse to eavesdrop on the people around me.

But today, the steps are more about stalling than anything, about staving off the memories that assault me every time I have played since Zaina died.

Sure enough, the memory hits with the first stroke of my bow.

My hair is loose, whipping around my face with each dramatic note of the song. I'm lost in the music, but not so lost that I don't see Mel dancing like she can erase all the ugliness of this place with the beauty in her fluid movements.

Maybe she can, but already, it seems I can't close my eyes without seeing the bloated, half-eaten carcasses that wash up to shore when the sharks are done with them. And those are just the lucky ones, the ones Mother didn't take time to deal with personally in her dungeons.

I drag my bow across the fiddle hard enough to make it screech before I move into another set.

Zaina is playing the piano in tune to my song. She's skilled enough at this, like she is at everything else, that she doesn't miss a note when I switch it up. But her eyes are even more hollow than usual, the bottoms sunken in from the days she's gone without eating.

Mother is so worried about her running away, I wonder if she's considered that Zaina might simply waste away instead.

I blink hard until the image is gone, swallowing the guilt that threatens to bowl me over. But even as I pick a jaunty song, one far removed from the memories of that day, I can't keep the thoughts from edging in.

The creeping suspicion that's been forming in my gut since Damian brought the news, the one that was cemented last night.

The way Zai's eyes were starting to get as empty as Mother's. The way she was constantly planning ten steps ahead, but somehow managed to die in a cave where she wasn't even supposed to be.

I don't know why, and I don't know how, but there is

increasingly less doubt in my mind that Zaina went to that cave to die.

🔥

I'm just placing my fiddle back in its velvet-lined case when I feel someone's eyes on me. I sigh and speak without even bothering to turn around.

"Have you come to haul me off in chains?"

Remy's black leather boots appear next to my fiddle case, and I intentionally take longer than necessary closing the clasps, giving myself time to school my expression.

"As tempting as the idea of you in chains is..." He lets that thought dangle in the air between us while he rakes his gaze over me. "I decided it would be more useful to follow you around until I stumble upon what I want to know."

"I knew you were bluffing," I reply, getting to my feet and slinging the strap of my fiddle's case over my back.

Remy is standing closer than I realized, my nose only inches from the brown tunic stretched across his broad chest.

Even now, even when the rest of me is hollowed out and raw, his closeness pulls at some forgotten part of myself, the part that almost feels human.

"If I didn't know any better, I would almost think you were upset about something." He reaches up to tuck a strand of hair back into my bun, sending an unwanted shiver down my spine. "But, of course, that would imply you have feelings."

"Let's not get ridiculous. I'm merely considering the imminent prospect of my untimely demise." I raise a single eyebrow, injecting a nonchalance I don't feel into my tone.

Before Remy can respond to my comment, a tiny figure scampers up to us. The child is too small to be Jessa, and she's the youngest person I have in my employ.

My eyes dart questioningly to the filthy face of what I'm fairly certain is a young boy. I might think he was here to pickpocket my earnings for the day, but mingled in with the dirt caked onto his cheeks is the unmistakable track of tears.

I lift his chin, studying him for any injuries while he looks back with fear in his eyes.

A group of nobles passes by with disgusted expressions, as if the child is rabid and might lash out at any moment. Remy shifts, turning us away from their prying eyes and gently guiding us to an alley near the cobblers.

Fresh, silent tears track down his face as I bend down again to get on his level.

"What is it?" Wariness sharpens my tone, and I try to will my face into something a bit softer.

The boy's blue eyes well up. "Jessa said — she said I should tell you, if—" He stops, sniffling.

I try for a gentler voice. "To tell me what?"

"If she dis—dis—a—"

Dread pools in my stomach, but it's Remy who speaks the damning word in a quiet, grim tone. "Disappeared?"

The boy nods, and I curse. It doesn't escape my grasp that in my work for Madame, I have contributed to this very situation.

And now another girl has been taken.

For some reason, images of Zaina flood my mind. Slavers didn't take her, but she was traded all the same while I did nothing to stop it from happening.

"Where did you last see her?" My tone is nowhere near gentle now. It's quiet, lethal, and already dripping with the promise of what will happen to the slavers I haven't had time to deal with yet.

Suddenly, I have all the time in the world.

a string of curse words flies through my head all the way to the bustling harbor, in part because Remy refuses to go away.

There isn't enough time to lose him, not if I want a chance at getting Zaina back, so I do my best to ignore him instead.

Jessa. If I want to get *Jessa* back.

Hundreds of ships are in the harbor, and several times that many people, but only one person I can be sure will have the information I need.

Even though Madame will hate that I'm coming here.

We pick our way through the crowded docks until I spy my contact in the usual place, hidden behind a fishing skiff that hasn't been touched in at least a decade. She's half immersed in the water, playing with the sea foam surrounding her, like a child would in a bath full of bubbles.

Remy's sharp intake of breath gives away his surprise at visiting one of the Mayima, likely because they generally disdain humans. But Natia is...different.

A board creaks under my foot, and her unnervingly bright silver eyes dart up to land on me. A wider grin sprawls across her full lips before she waves me over.

"Gemma!" she squeals. "How lovely to see you today."

Her smile fades as she gets a look at the man behind me, and her gaze stalks us the rest of the way down the dock. She slowly sinks further into the sea foam, only visible from the tip of her golden-brown nose up to her long, turquoise curls, as if she's ready to bolt at any moment.

Damn him.

"It's all right, Natia. He's a friend," I say, holding up my hands to show her we mean no harm.

It's a good thing that lying comes second nature to me, because that's the last word I would use to describe Remy at the moment.

"Oh, I'm a friend now, am I?" he says under his breath, and I resist the urge to elbow him in his perfectly chiseled abs.

"Not the time, halfwit," I whisper back.

Natia's head tilts to the side as she watches us. I've always marveled at how the Mayima can breathe underwater without gills or a spiracle. Other than their bright hair and wild eyes they seem human. Hell, with the fashion in Bondé being what it is, they would easily blend into the noble crowds on land if only they could breathe above the water for longer than a few minutes.

Natia's eyes are solely on me as if she's trying to read my expression.

"Where is the beautiful one?"

She asks this every time I visit and the question stabs at a raw, festering wound inside of me. I try and fail to shake the pain away.

"She's gone," I force the words out quickly, feeling rather than seeing Remy's probing stare. "Natia, we really can't stay long. We need this information now."

"You are upset," she says in her melodic, lilting accent, scooping up another handful of the sea foam and staring at me through the bubbles.

How astute.

"What do you know about children leaving the harbor?" I ask quickly, hoping to get to the point instead of the familiar song-and-dance routine we always find ourselves in.

"What is wrong?" she questions, diving under the water to take a breath. "I can feel your energy, and I do not like it." She shudders. "I do not think you like it, either."

Remy makes a grunt of agreement, and I roll my eyes.

We're running out of time.

The Mayima have a reputation of driving a hard bargain, usually to their benefit and to the detriment to the human who dares to agree to it. Working with Natia is difficult in an entirely different way, though, with the constant random shifts of her focus.

"Natia, this is important. Have you seen one of the ships taking children?"

She glances back and forth between Remy and me, but this time her eyes linger a bit longer on him. The corner of her mouth quirks up, and I turn in time to see Remy reciprocating it.

"Natia." I pull her attention back to me. "Please."

Her eyes snap back to mine, and it's as if a cloud has lifted from her.

"Oh! Yes! I have seen them." She pauses. "But this is not new information. Children are smuggled out to sea every day, and no one seems to care about them. Is this not a normal thing that humans do?" She says the words without accusation, only genuine curiosity.

Remy curses like he's surprised, and I suppress an eye roll at the bubble he insists on living in.

"Which. Ship." I bite out each word, trying to compel Natia to answer the question directly.

She takes a moment to think it over, tapping a finger on her chin.

"I don't know. It is difficult to keep track of all of you humans. So many coming and going from this harbor..." Her voice trails off.

Grabbing a minted gold coin from my bag, I hold it up and allow it to reflect the light. Natia gasps and swims closer.

"So shiny!" she says, her mouth stretching wide over her pearly white teeth.

"Natia, I will give you this coin if you can think really hard and try to remember who it was that you heard talking about the children. Or even if you just remember what they look like."

She nods excitedly before her face scrunches up in concentration. Several minutes pass before she claps her hands.

"Oh! I know! It was the men with the four black lines on their arms!"

I run through the known tattoos of the local crews until something clicks.

Sands-blasted hells.

"Did it look like this?" I ask, drawing the four rigid lines that make up the letter P in the sea foam she's been playing with.

Natia squeals in approval.

I toss her the gold coin and thank her, turning on my heels to leave. They aren't far from here.

That's the symbol of the Pillagers, Madame's most lucrative recent... acquisition. She won't be pleased to lose such a heavy source of income.

But I'm finding that I care less and less every day about what *pleases* Mother.

CHAPTER THIRTEEN

AIKA

*T*he tavern is packed. Smoke billows out from the doorway with each person who enters or leaves, ushering out sounds of the raucous celebration from within. Are they congratulating themselves on their latest haul of children? Anticipating the payoff that's coming?

My fingers itch toward my stars, but I remind myself we need something from them. We need them alive. For now.

"They almost look normal," Remy whispers, low enough that the men won't hear us from our spot on the roof.

"What did you think they would look like?" I respond in the same vein. "Were you expecting horns growing out of their heads? For some of them to have tails?"

He lifts a shoulder. "I really wasn't sure what to expect from the kind of monsters that could work for someone like *her*."

I fight the urge to scowl at being lumped in with the

despicable slavers, but at least I know what he would think of me if he ever found out the truth.

"This should be easy enough," I say, deliberately changing the subject.

He nods, staring down at the entrance of the tavern and counting the men entering under his breath. "A few rounds of ale should loosen their tongues."

"We don't have time for that," I argue. "Just follow my lead."

Ripping off my cloak and stuffing it into my satchel, I unlace the front of my undershirt before tugging it lower on my shoulders, imitating the style of the brothel girls.

Remy stares as I unpin my braid and adjust myself within the corset, trying to amplify the small assets I have.

Small flecks of snow flutter through the air, the first sign of winter's approach. A shiver runs through me as I shake out my braid, pulling the long waves around my shoulders to offer some small protection from the cold.

"Are you coming?" I ask, climbing over the parapet and down onto the ladder.

Remy curses under his breath before following me.

When we're on the ground, I shove my satchel into his hands and motion for him to go around the back, but I don't turn to look at him. Right now, I need to fight down the sinking, twisted feeling gnawing at my gut at having to interact with one of the Pillagers, no matter how brief it will be.

If it weren't for Jessa, I would light the entire tavern on fire right now and be rid of the lot of them.

I walk straight up to the window and pretend to use it as a mirror, polishing my lips with the deep red gloss I keep on me at all times. The men at the nearest table turn to me, drinking in every inch of my body from my head to my feet.

Bile rises in my throat, but I swallow it down as I stare at them seductively. My gaze flits between the men before I land on the one who looks like he would break the easiest.

It's always the biggest men, the ones used to being in control, who flounder when it's taken.

I follow the tattooed lines of his arm all the way up to his eyes and wink, hating myself when he responds with a feral grin. Maintaining eye contact, I gently bite the corner of my lower lip, then slowly make my way around the corner into the alleyway, knowing he'll follow.

After all, money is no object when they have just secured another payload.

I make a mental list of all the ways I could kill the man to pass the time in the few seconds before he opens the door, whistling to beckon me. Like I'm a dog.

"Over here," I say in the breathy tone of the pleasure-house women.

He enters the alleyway, and I'm suddenly grateful that wherever I wound up in life, it was not as a woman who actually would have had to put herself at the mercy of this barbarous man.

Not that I would be at his mercy with my skillset. The reminder that Remy is watching in the shadows is all that stays my hand from attacking the man now.

Playing a part is one thing. If I take down a grown man three times my size, Remy is sure to start asking questions I can't answer. So, I keep a grin plastered to my face as the Pillager stalks closer, following me around the back of the building into the alley.

"Don't tease me." His voice is higher pitched than I'd expect from a man his size.

"I wouldn't dream of it," I reply, running a hand through my hair.

Pausing, I allow him to come closer, to grip my waist with his calloused hands and pull me flush against him. His breath is rancid, heavy with the odor of spirits and tobacco, and it's an effort not to gag.

Self-loathing crashes over me as he roughly presses his mouth against mine. Every part of me rebels against the necessity of playing this role, but fortunately, Remy does his part quickly.

I hear a thunk as the man's eyes roll to the back of his head and his massive body drops to the ground.

Remy is standing behind him, face twisted in anger as he looks at the body in disgust.

"What's next?" he asks, wiping the stray specks of blood from the hilt of his sword.

"Next, we get our information." I start to head back the way we came when the banging sound of the door closing makes me curse under my breath.

All anyone would have to do is look around this corner to see their fallen comrade.

I exchange a quick, alarmed glance with Remy, my hand already twitching toward the false pocket where I stash my weapons. His gaze follows my movements before he pulls me around the corner and pushes me bodily against the wall, directly in the view of the newcomer.

I'm torn between yelling at him and killing the man approaching us when Remy presses his body against mine. He leans down, pausing when he is close enough for me to smell the residual notes of sage and lavender from his shaving balm, close enough for me to feel his breath on my lips.

The split second is long enough for me to stop him, if I want to.

But I don't.

Instead, I push up onto my toes to bring myself closer to him, the way I did a thousand times when we were together for reasons so much more complicated than an alibi.

His lips are soft and warm and gentle, but his kiss is none of those things. It's fire, powerful and all-consuming.

Even knowing that we hate each other, that there is death and torture in our very near future, and that there is nothing romantic about tracking down a revolting crew of slavers, my body reacts.

Lighting sizzles through every point of contact, my mouth molding against his like it was meant to be there. He makes a low, growling sound, moving his hands to the backs of my thighs as he lifts me, pulling my legs on either side of his waist.

My back hits the wall with an audible thunk, and I ignore it, fisting my hands in his hair.

For the show, I tell myself.

That also must be why his tongue grazes mine, why I open my mouth for him to explore more deeply. Why all I can feel is his rough stubble against my chin and his teeth on my lips and the ten points of his fingers digging into my thighs.

Vaguely, I register a sound that doesn't belong, but it takes me too long to place it as the voice of someone else.

"Hey!" The tone makes me realize it isn't the first time someone has tried to get our attention.

I blink. *Of course.* The man from the tavern. The entire reason we entered this charade.

Remy abruptly drops me, severing every point of contact. I barely catch myself from falling over before turning away like I'm embarrassed to be caught.

"Do you mind?" Remy's voice is annoyed.

"Came out to see what all the noise was," he answers in an uncertain voice and I'm relieved to see that it's not one of the men who were ogling me through the window.

"As you see." Remy is still out of breath, and it does things to me that it shouldn't.

"Well, take it somewhere else," the man says in a firmer tone. "This is a business establishment."

That pulls me out of whatever stupor I have temporarily sunken into. Business. *The business of trading children, you mean, you sick bastard.*

Remy huffs out a halfhearted apology and holds my waist while he backs away until my feet are firmly on the ground. Only when the man goes back inside do I brave a glance at Remy.

His lips are swollen, his eyes still slightly dazed, but all he says is, "Guess it's a good thing we're both familiar with a good bluff."

"Yes, I'm glad I've gotten so good at faking it when we're together." I can do nothing about the redness that creeps so easily from my neck into my cheeks, but at least my tone is dry.

With that, I stalk past him toward the unconscious form of the man, stopping only long enough to pick up my cloak. Remy's breathing is still ragged as he catches up to me.

Bluffing, my ass.

CHAPTER FOURTEEN
AIKA

e're both panting by the time we drag the man down the back alley into the abandoned fishmonger's shop a block away. There is a distinct trail in the sludge on the ground showcasing two sets of footprints dragging what is obviously a body.

I curse and tell Remy to go cover our tracks as soon as we're inside. Whatever small bit of amusement I had wrangled a few minutes ago has effectively evaporated in the wake of what I have to do now.

With practiced fingers, I tie the unconscious man to a chair, using a special reinforced bit of twine Mother helped me create. Every shred of emotion has left my body, replaced by the cool, detached calm I have cultivated for this very purpose.

So that I can get the job done.

I tie my hair back in a knot before pulling my favorite knife from my satchel, a deceptively delicate blade, then seat myself in front of the unconscious brute.

Before I can wake the man up, Remy reenters the shop. His gaze darts from the knife in my hand to the tied-up man, landing at last on my perfectly unperturbed features.

Rare emotion flickers in his eyes. Shock, maybe, with an edge of horror.

"What are you doing?" He rushes over, edging his body between the Pillager and me.

"Getting our answers." I say it like it's obvious, because it would be to anyone with any street sense at all.

"You can't torture him." He whispers the word *torture*, as if it's profanity, and I try to remember the version of me that Remy sees. A thief, a gambler, not someone with the expertise to kill or torture someone.

"It can't be that hard." I pretend to misunderstand what he's saying, but he doesn't buy it.

"You've done this before," he says flatly.

It's too close to things I've been actively trying to hide, but I won't very well be able to deny it when I start slicing the man up, either. I sigh, deciding on a watered-down version of the truth. My specialty.

"In another life."

His eyes bore into mine, every bit as intense as they were in the alleyway. But where there was desire before, now there is only a quiet disbelief.

"What exactly did you think we were going to do when I said we needed to get information out of him?" I am genuinely curious about this, though annoyance coats my words as well.

"Not this!" Remy hisses.

"No? Maybe you could try asking him nicely, when he regains consciousness. That should go splendidly."

"Wouldn't bribery be faster?" he counters.

"Bribery?" I grit the word out through clenched teeth.

Remy nods, and I shake my head in disgust.

"You want to give money to a man who steals children off the streets and *sells* them? Do you honestly think funding child trafficking is ethically superior to torturing a man who deals in it?"

His jaw ticks, and he bites out a curse. "You can't just expect me to stand here while you... slice him up, or whatever you're going to do."

"You're damned right I don't expect you to just stand there," I spit out. "You wanted to follow the trail of seedy underground criminals, were willing to risk your life and mine for it, so I expect you to be useful. You can help hold him down."

Remy looks at me like he's never seen me before.

He takes on the same expression he gets when he's counting cards or deciphering someone's line of play, only this time, he is appalled by whatever he has figured out.

Several heartbeats pass before he opens his mouth, probably to protest or ask more questions, and I cut him off.

"Or you can leave, and never again come tracking me down for help when you aren't willing to get your hands dirty for it." I wave toward the door.

Remy squeezes his eyes shut and shakes his head, but his feet stay firmly planted.

He doesn't even flinch when I wake the man with my knife.

Sweat breaks out over the man's head as I drag my blade across his skin for the hundredth time, but he doesn't scream. Not after the last time, when I made him pay for it.

"They call this the *lingering death*," I say calmly. "It's a method I've grown quite fond of. No one survives past a thousand, but they do usually tell me what I need to know by, oh, about a hundred and fifty. So tell me, sir, what is your magic number?"

I slice his arm again, this cut within a hair of the last. His skin may as well be butter for all the resistance it gives.

People are always so much more fragile than you expect them to be.

"I can pay you, anything you want," the slaver pants.

We've made it to the bribery stage even faster than I thought we would. It won't be long before he breaks.

Instead of responding, I tilt my mouth up in a macabre smile, letting him see how unaffected I am by his pain. It's more forced than usual, though.

I have been Madame's weapon for so long that torture has become as natural to me as breathing. I know where to cut or hit or stab to inflict the most pain. I know the quickest route to death and the most agonizingly slow one.

Usually, it's easy, each cut numbing me from the inside out. But then, usually, Remy isn't here, reminding me of whatever is left of the humanity still desperately trying to cling to my soul.

Remy stops in his pacing to ask the question again.

"Where. Are. The. Children?" He bites out each word more angrily than the last.

As angry as he is with the slaver, though, I suspect a good bit of that ire is directed at me, for being this person. At himself for allowing it to happen. It's a shame I've never had the luxury of his scruples.

I cut the man three more times in quick succession, and he groans loudly.

"All right! All right. Just make her stop," he says through ragged breaths, and I sit back, waiting for a location.

"They're bound for the southern continents. Labor camps pay good there." He takes a deep breath. "We sail under the black-and-red flag. Please, just stop."

From any other criminal's mouth, I might have an ounce of pity, but not for him. Not for a slaver.

His words are cut off as I make my final slash and effectively slice open his throat.

A dead man has no chance to warn the others we're coming. Killing him is the only way our plan has a prayer.

Remy curses and runs over to him, trying to stop the blood flow.

"I'm heading to the docks." My voice feels far away, like someone else is speaking. "I need to try to stop the ship before it's too late."

"Gemma—" Remy trails off, watching me clean the blood from my blade with the inside of my shirt.

He's staring at me like I'm the villain, rather than the man who steals and barters children for a living.

"None of them deserve to live. Besides, keeping him alive would only further their cause and make our lives a hell of a lot worse. Or did you forget that he saw both of our faces?" All at once, I tire of explaining myself.

I throw my cloak around my shoulders, stuffing the twine and weapons back into my bag.

"Are you coming with me to the harbor or not?"

"No, I'm not coming with you. I am going to get the guard who might actually be able to stop this." He runs a frustrated hand through his hair. "Unlike the two of us here, like this. Even if you are willing to torture everyone between here and the Eastern Lands." He mutters that last part, and I ignore it.

"Great. I'll head to the docks while you waste your time on that." I spin around, leaving him and whatever ill opinions he has of me behind as I run toward the last chance I have of saving Jessa.

CHAPTER FIFTEEN

AIKA

*T*he world around me fades to a blur as I race through the city streets and dark alleyways, my mind focused on the quickest route to the harbor.

There's still time.

There has to be.

The ships at port are always lined up in the direction they intend to sail, so I veer to the right, toward the southern docks.

There are still a solid fifty or sixty ships to search.

I increase my pace, my legs burning with the strain, until the frigid sea spray washes over me, and I can see the navigational lanterns lighting up the harbor. My eyes scan the flags of the ships, and I mentally check off the designs and colors.

None of them are red and black.

It should be here. *But it's not.*

Starting at the first ship again, I carefully rescan each one, but it's nowhere to be seen.

My heartbeats slow, each echoing ominously in my

head as I search farther out on the churning sea. Four ships sail in the distance.

No.

I grab the compact spyglass from my satchel, cursing as I pull it open and line it up with the ships on the horizon. The first one bears the mark of a normal trader. The second one is a flag I don't recognize, but the third…

No. No. No.

A red and black flag sways in the wind at least five miles out. Any morsel of hope I've had dissipates completely. I'm used to this, to children being possessions and sold or traded at will. I *should* be used to this.

But suddenly, I'm not.

Jessa's face is blending with the orphans I knew from my time on the streets and the children like her that I've known since then.

Then all I can see is Zaina, coming back from days of extra "training" with Mother, her face gaunt, her eyes guarded, and I'm left feeling even more hollow than before.

I failed her. I failed them both.

I curse as I throw the spyglass back into my bag, running a hand over my face.

She's gone. After all of that, Zai is gone.

Jessa. *Jessa* is gone.

And there is nothing I can do for either of them now.

A rush of icy air fills my lungs and coats me with more of the ocean mist. Somewhere in my mind, I register that I should be cold, but I barely feel the wind at all. Taking a steadying breath, I pull the hood of my cloak down low.

No, I can't help anyone now, but at least I can make the bastards pay.

There are a few stragglers still at the tavern. It isn't as packed as it was earlier, but there are at least sixteen of the Pillagers left inside.

Sneaking through the back with my hood still covering my face, I warn the few women working in the kitchen to leave. They stare at me with a mixture of fear and confusion, like they aren't sure whether I'm serious or not.

"Leave or die," I say bluntly, and they spring into action, signaling to the barmaid before they all take off down the alley.

When there is no one left inside but me and the Pillagers, I toss a large bottle of *skull thorn* through the kitchen door into the main room. It doesn't take long for the poison to activate, causing a fog to sweep through the area.

One by one, they fall, paralyzed, and eyes wide with fear.

Good. I hope they're half as terrified as their victims were.

When the fog dissipates, I enter the main room and remove a bottle of distilled turpentine from my satchel, sloshing it on the floors, the tables, and even the men.

Especially them.

Next, I walk a slow, taunting circle with a different bottle. This one is actually for containment, to keep the fire from spreading to the rest of the slums.

But the men don't know that.

"I'd wager you're all feeling rather helpless right about now," I croon to the slavers.

There are a few answering moans that I take to

mean yes.

"Good," I reply, staring down at one man in particular.

His eyes go wide with panic.

"I hope you feel just as defenseless as every single one of the children you stole and sold. I hope you remember each of their faces before you die."

There are several sharp intakes of breath, and more than a few tears.

"Can't do this." One upstanding gentleman manages to force a few words out, slowly. "Under Madame's protection. The Flame will come for you."

I walk over to him, leaning down close, whispering the last words he'll ever hear in a voice even colder than my dear *Mother's*.

"No." I shake my head. "The Flame has already come for you."

His eyes widen in shock, and I straighten out to finish my work.

The sobs start when I light my matchstick. They know who I am now.

They know that the vigilante leaves only ashes behind.

I would be lying if I said it doesn't give me a perverse pleasure, letting them in on my little secret just before I drop the match to the floor.

Flames roar to life, latching on to the trail of liquid all around the room. Then I walk calmly out of the tavern, closing the door behind me and leaving them to their fates.

Darkness settles over me like a thick blanket in the alley where I watch the building burn. A loud explosion sounds and another and another, with each bottle of liquor the flames come in contact with.

It's a shame, really, so much liquor going to waste.

I don't flinch as glass from the windows explode and rain down in the middle of the road. It's familiar now. A sound that reminds me that the men dying inside will never hurt anyone ever again.

Smoke billows from the windows and chimney, sending up a signal to anyone watching that I've been here. It's time to go.

My only regret is how quickly this will all be over.

They deserve so much worse.

But this is the only justice I can give Jessa.

I am turning away from the fire at last when movement from the shadows at the perimeter catches my eye.

Someone is coming.

I step farther back into the alleyway, ensuring that my hood covers my features from whoever is approaching. When the figure moves closer to the burning building, the dancing flames illuminate his grotesque features.

Sands-blasted hells.

Damian.

Did he follow me here? Does he know I'm the one he's been looking for?

Maybe it was the explosion that brought him here. Or maybe it was the smell of smoke.

I war with myself between fleeing and confronting him, but I risked enough with the fire. I can't risk being caught by Damian, too. Besides, the men inside should be dead by now. I can leave in peace, knowing that they paid for their crimes.

Or at least that there are a few less slavers in the world.

Reluctantly, I turn again to leave when another figure emerges from the shadows.

And this one is nearly as familiar as the first.

he emerald cloak and confident gait would have given Remy away, even if I didn't see the face hidden beneath his hood.

Stupid, stupid boy…

There are only a handful of moments before Damian will spot him.

Even if Damian doesn't think Remy is the vigilante, he might kill him to avoid having the crime pinned on himself.

Either way, there is no way Remy is walking out of here alive.

I massage my temples and curse beneath my breath. A small part of me, the part of me that works for Madame, insists that this could solve all of my problems at once. If Damian thinks he's put a stop to the fire-starter, then I won't have to worry about him investigating me anymore.

And if he takes out Remy… Well, that would eliminate the one person who suspects me, who saw me torture and murder a man tonight.

The logical thing would be to walk away.

But nothing about Remy and me has ever made sense.

My feet move before I can think better of it.

My cloak is pulled low over my face, hiding it from view as I pull a small, blue vial from my bag. I throw it to the ground, causing dense smoke to go up around all of us. When the two of them are coughing and struggling to see, I knee Damian in the groin and kick him toward the burning building.

I know it won't stop him, but it may buy us time. Then I head for Remy, grabbing his hand and pulling him through the alleys and back roads until I'm sure we're out of Damian's grasp.

I try to let go of his hand, but he holds fast, ripping my cloak back from my face.

He stares at me in the waning light of the moon, his eyes churning through a sea of emotions until his features completely harden.

"So, when you said you never hid who you were... that was what? Just an exaggeration?" He laughs, but the sound is entirely without humor.

"Please. Let's not pretend that either of us is known for our honesty." I don't quite scoff, but it's an effort.

"But it would seem that only one of us is known for burning people alive." He looks toward the inferno, then back at me. "You know I have no choice but to turn you in for this."

I'm not overly worried about that since I could easily break free of his hold on my wrist.

"Ah, yes. Where is your merry band of guards? Did they get lost in the slums? I hadn't realized they were even aware this part of the city existed." I don't bother to keep the acerbity out of my voice.

"Oh, you know. They were probably distracted by that

giant, raging fire you set." He sighs and runs his hands through his hair.

I narrow my eyes at him.

"Well, you were too late. The guards are always too late," I spit.

Then again, so am I. The thought assaults me, taunting me with its truth.

"Then why take out our only sources of information on where the ship went?" Remy asks.

I let out a bitter laugh, stepping closer to him. "There was no information to be had. The slavers don't share their routes, and by the time we tortured the answer out of any of them, it would have been impossible to catch the ship."

"Right, and why try to question people when you can just set them on fire instead?" He moves toward me, his furious breaths mingling with mine.

I stare up at him, disbelief darkening my voice. "Did you really think they deserved to live?" We are so close, our lips could be touching, when he answers me.

"Do you think that's up to you? That you are the one who gets to choose who lives and who dies?" His voice begins as little more than a whisper of air between us, but his grip on my wrist tightens. "How many people were in there? A dozen? More? How many souls have you taken today without a single shred of remorse?" His usual mask of calm is nowhere to be found tonight, and his voice raises uncharacteristically on that last word.

He doesn't know a bloody thing about my guilt, about the things I've done to deserve it.

"Oh, I have plenty of remorse, and every bit of it is for not ending them before they could steal and hurt more children," I hiss, wrenching my hand away from him.

"Don't forget who the real victims are here, Remy. Why don't you try applying your mercy to them?"

"Mercy isn't some finite resource, Gemma. Did you ever stop to think that not every person in that bar was even guilty? Maybe they had families, children."

A chill runs through me, his words sounding far too close to what Zaina would have said. The thought of her sobers me a little, and my next words come out softer.

"Don't fool yourself, Remy. We all have choices, and every person in that tavern chose to be there. When you decide to work with people like that, you get what's coming to you eventually."

I close my eyes, the words hitting a little too close to home. Before I can dwell any further on that, the faraway sound of the guards reaches us.

"Just in time to save the day." My voice drips with sarcasm. "I suppose that's my cue to leave. Oh, but feel free to fester in your own self-loathing at the wanton slaughter of an innocent band of child slavers." I turn to go, and Remy moves like he might stop me.

I raise my eyes to meet his in a silent challenge.

"I told you—" he starts, but I cut him off.

"I know what you said, but the fact is that you owe me a life. I just saved yours back there, in case you were too busy proselytizing to notice."

A heartbeat passes, and we both know I could kill him if I wanted to. We both know he could call out for the guards if he wanted to. Still, we stand deadlocked until he nods.

"Sure, Gemma. For old time's sake, then." He strives for his usual sarcastic tone, but it's coated in bitterness. "A life for a life. But next time—"

"Don't flatter yourself. There won't be a next time," I interrupt.

"Because you're going to stop?"

Everything in me balks at his question for reasons I can't quite understand. The reality is that I don't have much of a choice now that he knows who I am and Damian is on my trail, but I don't give him the satisfaction of admitting that.

"Because I'm not so easy to pin down."

"Don't I know." He says the words quietly, as if they're more for himself than for me.

Looking back, it seems like it was always inevitable that we would wind up here, on opposite sides of a city on fire. He is a guard, and I am one of the most notorious criminals in the kingdom. Everything we ever imagined between us was based on a game, on a series of crafted lies.

Even if it did feel real sometimes.

The pounding of footsteps thunders closer to the alleyway, and I take one last look at Remy, remembering the first night we met.

"Deal me in." The boy who's been watching me play all night finally meets my eyes, slapping his ante in the center of the table.

"Or I could save you the time and just take your coin now," I offer.

"And deprive you of your first interesting game of the night? I could never." He looks at the men seated on either side of the table before adding, "No offense."

And sands help me, I can't help the rare, genuine smile that spreads across my face.

He eyes me with undisguised intrigue and amusement, and I

know that even though I've been baiting him all night, even though I wanted him to come over here, this is a terrible idea.

And it's going to end badly.

I was right about that, at least.

As he holds my stare, I get the sense he's reliving that same night, or one of our many others. All traces of anger have vanished from his features, replaced with a sour sort of regret.

I think about the fundamental things he doesn't begin to understand, the things he's been too sheltered to notice or care about, and I can't help but return the sentiment.

Even if it hurts more than I'm willing to admit to myself to walk away from him again.

"Have a nice life, Remy."

CHAPTER SEVENTEEN
EINAR

I knew going into this that Khijhana would raise eyebrows, but I was unprepared for the terror and chaos she inspires at every inn.

This one is no different. Gunnar and Helga unload the trunk where Zaina hides, and the petite innkeeper rushes out.

"Sir, we welcome you, of course, but perhaps the other guests might be more comfortable if you had a lead for your…" She pauses, unsure of how to classify the chalyx. "Tiger?" Her expression is tight and narrow eyes assessing, as though she's taking in my obvious wealth and weighing it against the inconvenience of one of her guests getting eaten.

Though I can't see Zaina, the crackle of her wrath practically emanates from her trunk. I don't envy anyone who tries to chain Khijhana in my wife's presence.

At least we'll be at the palace in a couple of days, and they've received word of the chalyx ahead of time.

"I assure you, she's quite well-behaved as long as no one has any ill intentions toward me." I could swear

Khijhana's lips curl up in a feline grin while she sits innocently back on her haunches. "But of course, you'll be compensated for the extra hassle." I nod to Gunnar, who steps forward with a heavy purse.

Just like with the past two inns, the heavy exchange of coins solves the problem.

The woman takes the purse. "Right this way."

She leads us into the building, barking orders at her workers in quick succession. Everyone straightens and stares at us with curiosity, and it's a relief when we're alone in the sizable suites.

All traces of my earlier amusement vanish when I help Zaina out of the trunk and see the pinched expression she tries to hide.

She catches the look on my face and immediately hardens her own.

I wonder if she'll ever stop feeling the need to hide herself, or if Ulla has so firmly ingrained it in her that it's just an intrinsic part of who she is now. It's a good quality in a queen, at least, even if I hate it for her.

"Did you hear the other guests talking about another fire?" she asks abruptly, running her hand over Khijhana's fur in continuous, automatic motions.

I nod. I had heard on the way up to our room, but she seems more interested in the news than I am. "Do you think *she's* behind it?"

Zaina shakes her head. "Arson doesn't feel like her. But it is interesting…" She leaves her spot by Khijhana to grab today's newspaper from the table, something far more common in Corentin than Jokith.

She scans the headlines until she finds the article she's looking for. When she's finished reading it, her shoulders stiffen and her brows knit together.

"What is it?" I ask.

She shakes her head again. "It's probably nothing, just warring factions trying to take each other out."

Uncertainty laces her tone, but I don't push it. I've been wondering about a few things as well.

"What do you know about the royals?" I ask. "From what I remember of the king, he doesn't seem the type to work with someone like Madame, but I only met the queen once." I sink onto the foot of the bed.

"When did you last see him?"

Before Ulla came along to rob me of all of my relationships, political or otherwise. "Nearly twenty years ago."

"People change in that amount of time," Zaina says softly, setting down the newspaper.

The turmoil churning in her eyes is more than I would expect for a relative stranger to her, and I wonder if she's thinking about more than just the king.

In twenty years, will she change while I remain largely the same?

Jokithans live to be several hundred years old, but no one knows exactly why, only that it's tied to the land somehow. The vague explanation never bothered me before I realized it was the difference in whether or not I would have to watch Zaina die one day.

Then again, if we can't come up with a way to stop Ulla, neither of our lives is likely to be very long.

"I know that," I tell her evenly.

She nods, but her face is neutral enough that I'm still not sure we're talking about the same thing. "I only know them in passing. The queen is friends with Lady Delmara, but she wouldn't be if she knew her "friend" was responsible for what happened to the crown prince. The whole family has been reclusive since then, but the king especially seems to have retreated."

Zaina crosses her arms over her chest and Khijhana presses her massive head to Zaina's leg, a sign that she recognizes the stress in her as well as I do.

"She killed the crown prince?" It shouldn't surprise me.

I have a vague recollection of a boy with curly brown hair teetering around his father's legs. And now he's dead, because of her.

"I suspect so." Zaina traces the navy stripes on Khijhana's head subconsciously. "She was furious that he married before she had the chance to orchestrate it to her advantage."

"And now the younger brother is up for marriage." His masquerade ball is on the front page of every newspaper we've seen.

"Well, that's one way to get close to the royal family. Perhaps it would give us an edge on Madame?"

Even knowing she's joking, I can't suppress a scowl at the idea of her with another man. "Indeed."

She gives me the barest hint of a smirk. "I must confess my weakness for gangly, pustule-faced boys who flirt with all the courtiers. It's truly a shame I'm both married and dead."

A small answering smile forms on my lips, but it's chased away by a frustrated growl. "What does she have to gain from ruining the lives of every monarch she can get her hands on?"

I'm talking to myself as much as Zaina, but she responds anyway.

"Besides the obvious, you mean?"

I shake my head. "She has wealth and influence

already, and even she has to have loftier aspirations than power for power's sake. What does she plan to do with it all? What is she really after?" I pinch the bridge of my nose between my forefinger and thumb, trying to dull the headache forming between my eyes.

These are questions we've asked before, questions without easily discernible answers. Instead of the clear lines of play I see in a chess game, everything looks murky from here.

Zaina shakes her head after a moment, looking as frustrated as I feel. She crosses the room to stand just in front of me, and I wrap my arms around her waist.

"I honestly don't know. I suppose that's what we're here to find out."

CHAPTER EIGHTEEN
AIKA

*a*n unearthly scream wrenches me from a fitful sleep.

It's been three days since I set fire to the Pillagers and left Remy in an alley in the slums. Being stuck at Mother's estate was almost a relief, almost a peaceful respite from the events of that day.

Until now.

Another shrill scream rings out, and I recognize the voice as Mother's.

Damn it.

Throwing on my robe, I dash out of the room and down the marble staircase, heading straight toward her chambers. The maids are scurrying away as quickly as possible, and I gesture for them to head toward the kitchens. They'll be safer there from whatever is going on in this room.

I push open the door, my dagger at the ready as Mother screams again.

My eyes scan the room, desperate for any clues that might have caused this reaction from her. Then I move closer to assess her for any sign of an injury. There's nothing.

"Did something happen?" I ask cautiously, preparing to subtly flee the room if she appears to be on the murder path again.

She turns on me, a letter in her hand, her violet eyes a tempest of fury so deep I'm not even sure she really sees me. Only Zaina's death has ever had the power to unhinge her this way. A dark thought crosses my mind.

"Is it Mel?" The words come out raspy.

"What? Of course not." Disgust joins her maelstrom of rage, like I should have known better than to think she would be upset by anything so trivial as her actual daughter.

"It just doesn't make sense," Mother continues, her hand flying to her temple, her long, elegant fingers pressing in. "How could *all* of them be cured? Where did he find the flowers?"

She appears to be talking more to herself, so I am contemplating creeping back out of the room when she finally, truly, notices me.

"When Einar gets here, I need you to find out everything you can about his visit, what he's here for, what he's brought with him. I need to know *everything.*"

I don't miss the oddly familiar way she says his name, but I give her the only response I can.

"Of course."

Mother has her hands in so many machinations, I don't bother to guess at what she's talking about.

I'm not even sure I want to know what she's planning these days.

🔥

I hide in my room for the rest of the morning, though I have to wonder if Mother's anger would be preferable to the time alone with my thoughts.

Or worse, alone with Mel's letter.

Mother sent a ship to deliver the news, and this note had arrived only days later, just before the waters became completely impassable. I've only read it once, but the words in her elegant script have been branded on my mind.

I miss her, she had written. *And lately, I'm afraid I'm going to have to miss you, too. I'm afraid that you're losing yourself, that her death will only make that worse. Stay with me. We're all we have now.*

My eyes close like I can shut out the words I'm reading by memory as easily as if I were examining the page.

Mel is brave. She doesn't hide from her feelings the way I do. The way Zai did. And maybe it's that kind of strength that makes me feel so weak by comparison.

Sands.

How had she seen even then, even before Zaina died, that things were spiraling out of my control?

I'm already headed toward the door when I answer my question from earlier. Facing Mother is a better alternative than sitting here with my own spiraling thoughts. I've no sooner placed my hand on the doorknob than my door pushes open.

Only my fast reflexes keep me from being knocked to the ground when Mother glides in, leading a group of women carrying several large trunks between them.

"Mother?" I ask hesitantly, the scene from earlier still fresh on my mind.

"Have you forgotten about your fitting for the ball already, Aika?" She wraps her arm around me in an outward display of affection. "And here you were so excited."

I follow her lead seamlessly, though we both know she never told me about a fitting today, only that I needed to stay here. "How silly of me. Of course, that's today. I can hardly wait to see what you ladies have in store." I beam at them, shooting eager glances toward the trunks I would just as soon set on fire.

The women respond in kind, chattering excitedly about their thoughts for my dresses and masks and what everyone else will be wearing so that we can avoid those styles while they pull the dresses from where they've been carefully packed.

All these years, even at court functions, I have dressed to blend in. Dark shades of navy and emerald and even gray allowed me to move around without much notice.

This time, though, the seamstresses parade bright, attention-grabbing hues in slinky fabrics that have irides-cent shimmers or even outright sparkle in the bright light of the chandelier.

Apparently, Mother has already had a dozen dresses made to my measurements, though I only need a few.

"We definitely want bold for the first night," she commands, and I find myself being shoved into one of the many gowns.

The ball is three nights, with the wedding taking place at midnight on the third one. Only serious contenders put their name in for consideration, since even volunteering is considered binding.

It wouldn't do for the prince to be turned down.

All of this so the spoiled halfwit can choose a wife the same way he would pick out the plumpest pheasant for dinner. I nearly scowl before I catch Mother scrutinizing me in the deep orange gown that's too fitted to fight in and the matching fox mask that interferes with my line of vision.

I don't bother to give my opinion. If it were up to me, I would wear black to mourn my impending marriage.

When Mother told me I had to marry the prince, it felt removed from me. Temporary, somehow. But now that the masquerade is only three nights away, I have to wonder how I will ever find a way out of this.

Does she intend for me to stay married to the prince forever? More likely, until she has me *dispose of him*. It shouldn't bother me, not when bloodshed and death are so common in my world.

Still, I see Remy's bitter, disappointed stare when he came face-to-face with my life as the vigilante. I hear him telling me that it's not for me to decide who lives or dies, and suddenly, the memories are suffocating me as surely as this sands-blasted corset does.

I want answers. Need them.

But after this morning, asking Mother anything feels like a risk that isn't worth taking.

Even for me.

CHAPTER NINETEEN
AIKA

*N*o sooner had the seamstresses removed my last gown than Mother was privately ushering me out the door with strict orders to find out why the Jokithan King has come to Corentin.

I don't mind because that's something I would also like to find out, but more than that, I can kill two birds with one stone. What better place to find out information about my future husband than the palace?

Still, it's odd that she's so concerned about King Einar's arrival. Maybe I'm not the only one who suspects he knows more than he lets on about Zaina's death. Either way, I intend to find out.

The walk to the palace is short, almost refreshing in the early winter chill. I use the distraction of the tolling bell thundering through the palace courtyard to sneak across the grounds. There's a tucked away section of the castle with thick, sturdy vines perfect for scaling.

Tiny snowflakes fall around me, making the climb far more slippery than I would prefer. In the warmer months, the palace is easy to sneak into, with all of the green vines and cherry blossom trees and lush gardens of the court-yard to hide behind.

Today, I'm just fortunate that the collective attention of the guards is on the palace gates.

Once I've climbed as far as the vines will take me, I use the small notches in the bricks to finish my way up to the turret roof to overlook the grounds below. Then I wait.

If I hadn't known Einar was arriving today, I might have missed it entirely.

He doesn't come with the usual fanfare of a king, even if the horses pulling his carriage are twice the size of the Corentine destriers. There's no contingent accompanying him, only two guards, one as dark as the other is fair. They both move with the fluid grace of highly trained warriors.

More intriguing still, one of them is a woman.

He's either cocky or stupid, coming to a foreign land with so little protection. *Or both.*

My eyes scan the vast welcoming crowd as the carriage rolls to a stop. Even the Corentine king has come personally to greet King Einar, though he leans heavily on a golden cane. His wife Queen Katriane is at his side, wearing an expression of sympathy before the Jokithan King even steps out of the carriage.

No sign of my future husband, though. He's likely too busy being fed from a golden spoon and trying not to run from his own shadow.

I watch with the rest of the crowd as a footman opens his carriage door, then promptly skitters back, as an enor-mous feline of some sort jumps out of the carriage. Not quite a tiger — not like any I've seen, at least — with its shimmering white fur, tall, pointed ears, and navy stripes lining its entire body.

It's beautiful, and terrifying, and I concede that the king needs no more protection than the creature offers.

The king himself follows. I can't help but hold my breath, like I can unravel the mystery of the last few months just by looking at him.

He is a beast of a man, taller even than his guards, with massively broad shoulders. He wears an axe at his back that I'm willing to bet is for more than show, and on his white-blond braids rests a silver, pointed crown. Not that he would need it, necessarily.

He is every inch a king, even without the accessory.

There isn't a single visible hint about why this man drove my sister to want to die rather than spend a lifetime at his side.

Then again, what did I expect? A confession nailed to his head?

I glance at the other two guards. In their body language with each other and the cat and even the king, it's apparent that there is a camaraderie between them all. Did they feel that way with my sister, too?

It's unexpectedly painful, looking at these strangers and knowing she spent her last few months in this world with them. I shove the feeling down, searching for some level of the numbness that has gotten me through the past few weeks.

The guards unload a nondescript trunk from his carriage, something I wouldn't have looked twice at were it not for the oddity of the situation.

There are footmen waiting to do that, which would keep his guards free to defend him. The palace staff offer to take it from them, but when their hands stretch out, the giant cat snarls softly.

Einar shakes his head, directing them to the trunks on

the outside instead, and the whole affair is forgotten as King Jean clasps wrists with King Einar before directing him into the palace.

Forgotten by them, anyway. But I need to know what's inside the trunk that's worth shielding when he didn't bother to protect his own wife.

I'm left with no choice but to visit the palace this evening.

CHAPTER TWENTY
EINAR

a knock sounds at the door as soon as we've unpacked the few items we brought with us.

Zaina has hidden herself before I turn around. The only reason I even know that she's in the closet is because Khijhana paws at the door before curling into a massive protective ball in front of it.

I nod for Gunnar to answer the door, and he returns seconds later with a note in his hand. Zaina appears next to me on silent footsteps, peering over my bicep at the letter in my hand.

A game of chess and a glass of whiskey before dinner, my friend?

-Jean

"You should go," Zaina says, studying my expression. "I'll be fine here."

I hesitate, stalling by carefully folding the paper and placing it in my pocket.

I wish that things were different and that she was coming with me. That I could introduce her as my queen to a very old friend.

I shake the thought away. There are far more important things to worry about than whether or not my bride can walk beside me publicly. She's right. I should go.

Even if it does mean leaving her side in the city where the most vile woman in the world resides.

Something in the softening of her eyes makes me wonder if she can sense what I was thinking, but if so, she doesn't say. She only stretches up on her toes, and I lean down to meet her parted lips with a kiss.

Within minutes, I'm following the familiar red-and-gold-lined rug toward King Jean's private room.

The portrait of Jean's father on the wall marks the passageway, and I move my fingers along the panel behind the frame until I feel the latch. When I push it to the right, the lock silently gives way, allowing me to move the wall inward.

The room where we spent late nights playing chess and talking politics so many years ago is exactly the same, down to its crystal decanter.

Only the man sitting by the fire has changed.

Jean stares into the flames, his eyes glazed over and far away, unlike the alert man I knew before. His hair has grayed, and his spine is hunched forward as if the actual weight of his kingdom is resting on his back.

I know the feeling.

"Hello, old friend," I say, approaching him.

Jean's head snaps up, finally free from whatever memory he had been lost in.

"It has been too long, Einar." His weathered hand reaches out for mine, and I take it gladly.

"And you haven't aged a day."

"Liar." He chuckles, gesturing toward a servant in the corner of the room.

The man comes forward and pours us both a dram of whiskey before returning to his station. His watchful gaze rests on Jean's trembling fingers when he passes him the drink, as if the king may drop it at any moment.

"How are you, Jean?" I ask in a more serious tone than before.

His eyes go distant again, and I wonder if he will answer me at all. I set the pieces up on the chessboard, prepared to drop the matter when he answers.

"Time has sunk it's filthy claws into me, my friend. My body and my mind aren't what they used to be. So much has changed..." He trails off, taking a sip of the whiskey. "But you, well, you look the same as you did twenty years ago. What I wouldn't give for that fabled Jokithan fountain of youth."

This time, his smile is bittersweet, and a pang of guilt jolts through me.

It's hard to reconcile what I see now with who I knew before. I've spent so much time shut away in Jokith that I've nearly forgotten how the rest of the world ages.

Memories flit through my mind quicker than lightning. My first visit to Corentin as a child with my parents, back when Jean was heir and I was just another prince. He taught me to play cards, and I taught him to play chess.

Then later, I was a grieving young king, and Jean followed me only a decade after.

The last time I saw him was nearly twenty years ago, when I met his first child. The boy who is now dead.

If I had been successful in finding Ulla, he would still be alive. Instead, I spent seventeen years trying to undo the damage she caused in Jokith while she ran off to wreak havoc in this part of the world.

"I am sorry about Louis," I offer quietly, and Jean's shoulders sink a little further.

"And I am sorry about your young wife," he says somberly. "Especially after all you have suffered."

There's a gleam in his eye I can't quite read. I wrote Jean with the same story about the plague that swept through Castle Alfhild, but a part of me always wondered how much of that he believed.

"What I wouldn't give to close the walls of Etienne and be done with the rest of the world."

"You don't mean that." I chuckle, but he nods adamantly.

"I do. You will find that I have become bitter in my old age, Einar. Being king has cost me everything. My health. My sanity. My son—" His voice cracks slightly on the last word before he downs the rest of his whiskey. "Besides, Katriane seems to have everything in order. The Lady Delmara has been a great help to her."

He says her name with an air of respect, and my heartbeat thunders in my ears.

His son is dead because of her, and I can't so much as do him the decency of letting him know. He would go after her, and she would either kill him or flee.

Or both.

If he even believed me.

Still, if I were in his position now and ever found out the truth, I would hate me for keeping it a secret.

I stew on that and my own guilt while Jean directs his attention to the board, gently spinning it so that the white pawns are in front of me. His fingers trace the pointed edge of the ebony king for a long moment before he speaks again.

"I am giving the throne to my son."

I glance up sharply. In Jokith, it's not uncommon for monarchs to retire early, but Corentine kings rule until death. He said he was old and tired, but I can't help but sense Ulla's hand in this.

"Does Katriane agree?" I ask carefully, trying to gauge whether Ulla might be swaying her.

"By the stars, no. It's like she thinks the throne will make Francis more of a target." Jean sighs. "She hardly lets the children outside of the castle since Louis."

I'm ready to admit I was hasty in assuming this was Ulla's work when he speaks again.

"But Lady Delmara is helping me persuade her. She's the one who finally convinced Katriane to host the masquerade for our son."

A muscle ticks in my jaw, and I'm grateful that Jean is too busy signaling for another whiskey to notice.

Ulla would never go to the trouble to orchestrate the heir's marriage and subsequent rise to the throne unless she had a candidate in mind.

Zaina is going to be furious.

CHAPTER TWENTY-ONE
AIKA

*T*his maid's uniform was not designed for scaling balconies.

When the royal party went inside, I had gone to seek out a better disguise to explore first the Jokithan King's suites, then those belonging to Prince Francis.

Knocking out Einar's guard would have raised an alarm, so my only option was stealth. The suites next to his were unlocked, and then it was a simple matter of shimmying along the ledge between this balcony and his.

Or, it would be, but the servant I pilfered this dress from was a solid few inches taller than I am.

I don't turn back, though, because this is the only time I know for sure the king will be out of his rooms. There's a customary welcome dinner the first night of any royal visit, and he wouldn't give offense by missing it.

The real gamble is whether or not he took the giant cat.

My foot creeps along the icy ledge, and the adrenaline rush of being suspended several stories up helps me clear my head. I take a calming breath.

The beast stayed close to his side on the way into the palace, without a chain of any kind, which makes me believe it's a companion animal of sorts.

In any case, he would hardly leave it in the rooms if it was liable to eat an unsuspecting maid.

Probably.

Nothing for it, though. I need to know what was in that trunk, and Mother instructed me to find everything I could on the king.

I leap the last few feet to the king's balcony. The handle to the door is locked, and I begrudgingly raise my respect for him a bit. No one thinks to lock the outer doors of a third-floor suite.

Still, picking these is child's play. I only need to use one hairpin.

As soon as I hear the click of the tumbler, I ease open the grand French doors of the balcony and poke my head inside. The main room is almost as opulent as Mother's estate, but I don't take time to admire the gold-embossed crown molding.

Instead, I search the vast space for signs of the cat.

"Kitty…" I call softly, but nothing stirs.

The prickling sensation of eyes on me follows each cautious footstep as I make my way into the room, leaving the door open.

As soon as I'm away from the doorway, the smell hits me.

Jasmine and cloves and something entirely Zaina.

I take a deep breath, wondering if my mind is playing tricks on me. It's faint, barely even there, but I would know that scent anywhere.

My breaths come faster, and I realize that I am not half as prepared for this moment as I thought I was.

I have spent weeks avoiding her bedroom, the training room, anywhere traces of her linger. *Why is it here?*

Has he brought back some of her things?

And what is the king even doing here in Corentin, when she must have hated him? Did she play her part that well?

The Zaina I knew couldn't have, not entirely. The fury burning in her caramel-colored eyes always gave her away.

I remember it well from the day I came to live with Mother, and the weeks that followed. The way Zaina's eyes would blaze every time she spotted me, even while the rest of her features were carved into bland perfection.

Eventually, that anger gave way to something softer.

And then it turned to emptiness, sadder and stiller than the kind Mother holds.

I try to shake off the memories, the guilt, the grief threatening to overtake me, heading for the trunk the king had protected earlier. It's bigger than the others, and not quite as ornate on the outside, almost as if it was designed to blend in.

That would have made me suspicious, even if I hadn't been watching his arrival.

It doesn't have a lock, though, which strikes me as odd, considering he clearly finds it important. I flip the lid open, only to find it's... empty.

The velvet cushioned lining is at odds with the plainer exterior, and I know — I know that something was in here. Something important. The jasmine smell is stronger here, but if it held my sister's things, why did he empty it already?

Or am I overthinking this, and it merely held gifts for the royals who were hosting him?

I'm so caught up in running my hands along the insides, searching for any signs I might have overlooked, that I nearly miss the soft patter of a large, agile creature slinking its way between me and the door.

My mind goes numb with the kind of fear I wasn't sure I was capable of anymore, my heart beating an unsteady rhythm in my ears. I only have time for one thought as I slowly turn around.

I was wrong about the cat.

CHAPTER TWENTY-TWO
ZAINA

*M*y senses are on alert before I even hear the scraping of metal on the balcony door — the sound of a lock being picked.

Helga went to dinner with Einar, and Gunnar is standing guard outside the main door. So, I retreat into the bedroom where Khijhana is napping to spy on whoever is desperate or foolish enough to break into Einar's room.

The answer shouldn't surprise me.

And it doesn't, really.

Seeing Aika's face, though... that's something else entirely. The day I went to the caves expecting to die, I resigned myself to never seeing my sisters again. Part of me still obstinately refused to hope, even as we embarked on the journey here.

Now that Aika is standing not twenty feet from me, lines of fatigue etched around her wide, angular eyes that weren't there before, I can't remember how to breathe.

She's alive.

For now, anyway. Not for long, climbing on icy

balconies in a fitted dress and risking the wrath of a chalyx.

What is she thinking?

She pauses in the doorway, looking almost... lost. She's so small, several inches shorter than I am. Suddenly, I don't want to involve her in any of this, even though I know that isn't reasonable. She's in it already, as steeped as she is in her role for Madame.

Every part of me longs to go to her, but I'm not ready.

Not like this. Not when I know nothing about what the last few months have brought for her or what she's doing now.

Not when I don't know if she will take my side or Madame's.

I nearly curse when she goes to the trunk. I told Einar not to worry if the footmen tried to carry me. It would have been difficult to brace myself for the trek to the room, but not impossible.

He and Khijhana couldn't help themselves, though, and of course, my sister noticed the odd behavior. That doesn't tell me whether she's here for her own sake or for Madame's, though the latter is far more likely.

Still, I want to talk to her without prying ears, and this might be my only chance.

I am so engrossed in warring with myself that I don't notice when Khijhana stalks from behind me, curious about this new intruder. Aika doesn't notice either, which is unusual enough.

I can't call Khijha back to me without alerting my sister, but I doubt she'll hurt anyone who doesn't mean me any harm. I wait, ready to step in, while Aika turns slowly around.

She freezes, her eyes landing on my chalyx.

Khijhana takes her in, the disparate pieces of my life colliding in one unlikely moment. It seems strange that two of the most important things to me know nothing about each other. Bone-deep sadness spreads through me as they gauge one another.

Khijhana catches my mood, making a high-pitched sound that represents everything going through my mind. She turns to go, and Aika takes her chance to leave.

The opportunity to talk to my sister is gone in an instant, and I'm left wondering if I made the right choice to stay hidden.

Sands, with the way she's acting and the chances she's taking, I wonder if she'll get herself killed before I get another chance.

CHAPTER TWENTY-THREE

AIKA

*J*asmine.

It's in my hair, on my clothes, clinging to every inch of me and threatening to drown me in memories of my dead sister.

Worse still, it's all I have to show for my ill-fated journey into the king's rooms.

That, and a heartbeat that still hasn't slowed from the near-death moment with the giant cat.

All of it was enough to temporarily quell my curiosity about the prince. I keep up a rapid pace all the way back to the estate, turning the encounter over in my head and trying to make sense of it.

Obviously, I was wrong about the king not leaving the beast in his rooms unattended. What was strange was the thing's odd cry at the end, like it was... sad.

Does it miss my sister? Did it somehow know I was connected to her?

I head straight for the bathroom, determined to wash off the visceral reminder of memories that threaten to drag me under.

Zaina, coming to my room the morning after my virginity was sold, bringing a tonic and a warm compress.

She doesn't speak, doesn't iterate the helpless fury that burns in her gaze. She only sets the things on my bedside, then presses her forehead against mine in a rare gesture of affection.

Her hair pools around me, shielding me from the room outside, and a waft of jasmine fills me with... something, too much, when I need to be numb and forget last night ever happened.

I pull back, scoffing.

"You're so dramatic, Zai. It was hardly the worst night of my life."

She shakes her head, uncharacteristic melancholy passing into her gaze. "That isn't better, A."

She gives me one last look before leaving me with the solitude I desperately need.

But the scent of jasmine remains, and I finally put a name to the feeling it gives me.

Comfort.

It isn't comforting now. It's like torture, slower and more excruciating than anything my knife could exact.

It's like she's died all over again.

What was I even expecting to find in that trunk? Some locked-away memory of how she spent those final months? My sister herself popping out, alive and well and proclaiming the entire thing a huge joke?

I scoff at myself. Zai was many things, many complicated things, but cruel was never one of them. If she were alive, she would have found a way to let Mel and me know.

If she were alive, Damian wouldn't have returned to Mother without her.

Logically, I never really thought there was a chance

otherwise. So why does it feel like I'm being crushed under the weight of a thousand corpses?

I don't wait for the servants to light the fire underneath the tub. Instead, I get in when the water is still cold from the tap and grab my roughest sponge, scrubbing harshly at my skin.

To hell with jasmine.

🔥

I am still drying off from the tub when a servant arrives with an invitation for me to join my mother for a meal.

A tremor runs through me, freezing my bones from the inside out.

In the ten years since she plucked me off the streets to offer me a life and a family and a purpose, Mother has never once asked me to dinner. Normally, she eats alone in the vast room that feels more like a tomb, pristine to the point of being lifeless.

But nothing has been normal since Zaina died.

I lace up my dress with numb fingers and hurry downstairs before she might consider me late.

The hearth is empty when I reach the dining hall, the air frigid and stale, but Mother sits unperturbed in a sleeveless evening gown. Attendants stand at the ready around the room, eager to acquiesce to her every demand. Or terrified not to, anyway.

A servant girl places an ornate plate in front of me with trembling fingers, either from the biting temperature or Mother's predatory gaze.

I don't blame her.

My heartbeat stutters in my chest, and the muscles in my face ache with the effort of keeping my expression bland while I survey my boiled chicken and vegetables for any signs of poison.

The room is heavy with the weight of expectation, like the tenuous seconds before the first strum of an instrument, but neither of us speaks.

Has she found out I'm the vigilante? Is this punishment, or merely a test?

It's a gamble, like everything else in my life.

But only a fool would try to call Mother's bluff.

Spearing a bite of chicken with my fork, I place it cautiously into my mouth, chewing slowly.

She doesn't move, doesn't touch her own food. Just as when I was standing off against the chalyx this afternoon, I am acutely aware that one wrong move may be my last.

Ignoring the way my blood roars in my ears, I make myself swallow.

But I don't breathe, not until she grants me an approving nod.

"You're less reckless than you used to be."

"Thank you, Mother." I incline my head. "You've taught me well."

Her smile widens. "Tell me what you learned today, Daughter."

Just like that, whatever twisted game she was playing has come to an interlude, leaving me to wonder if I imagined the entire thing.

I take another breath before I recount my experience in the king's rooms, sticking closely to facts rather than revealing what effect the visit had on me.

"So, you gleaned nothing from this?" She grips her chalice in white knuckles, the only outward sign of her aggravation.

"No," I admit, swallowing down another wave of apprehension. "I had to leave because of the beast."

"Odd that he left it alone…" She trails off thoughtfully. "In any case, I, at least, managed to gather some useful information. Einar is coming here tomorrow."

Ignoring her jab, I take another bite of my bland chicken.

"And you would like me to be here to greet him?" It's the obvious choice, me playing courtier.

"No," she all but snaps.

My eyes fly to her face.

Something in her expression is off, so subtle that I almost miss it.

Is that why she's called me here, to ensure I'm just distracted enough to miss whatever she's keeping from me about the king?

"You may casually acknowledge him," she allows. "Speak with him in front of others, but that is it."

None of this makes sense.

If she wants to know more about Zaina's time there, and what really happened, shouldn't she want me to get close to him?

A breath later, she adds, "The queen and I have an arrangement. It would do irreparable damage if she believed you had designs on the newly eligible king."

I blink. Not because she has an arrangement with the queen — that much I had assumed. Otherwise, she would have no way of expecting me to marry the prince.

But the idea that I would wed the man my sister was forced to marry is unthinkable, even if it is a common enough custom here.

"I won't have Einar ruining my carefully laid plans."

Once again, I'm compelled to wonder if I'm reading

too much into all of this, seeing things that aren't there when Mother is merely scheming the same way she always has.

"Of course." I keep my voice bland, though my mind is racing.

Maybe she isn't hiding anything, but that doesn't mean the king doesn't have information I need.

I should leave it alone, considering how close I have come to risking her wrath in the past few weeks, but I can't.

I have to talk to the king.

CHAPTER TWENTY-FOUR
EINAR

I am fighting to control my temper from the moment I walk through the doors of the Delmara Estate.

I scoff internally. There never was a Lord Delmara, from what Zaina tells me. Just a mountain of money to buy this property off a floundering lord, and an island small enough that no one questions who hails from it.

Just one more thing she's fabricated. Like her family. Like her humanity.

Where Palais de Etienne is all light and open and inviting, Ulla's estate is the opposite.

It's all sharp columns and detailed mosaic windows that are busier than any other structure I have seen in Corentin, or even Jokith. All of this, coupled with the newer-looking beastly statues on the roof, lend the entire building a gothic feel that is more popular in the southern continents.

Taking a breath, I nod to the servants standing outside to greet Khijha and me, forcing something resembling a smile onto my face. The only person missing from the welcoming party is Ulla herself. No sooner has the thought crossed my mind than one of the servants leads me into the estate and to a room with broad, closed doors.

"She's right through there, Your Majesty. We were instructed to give you privacy." The man leaves without opening the door for me.

Odd.

As soon as I enter the room, I see why. It's been seventeen years since I've laid eyes on Ulla, but her deep brown skin, tightly coiled purple curls, and violet eyes are seared into my memory.

The woman sitting before me now has none of those things.

Her skin is lightly tanned under what I suspect is a wig of sleek-black hair, and her eyes are a golden shade eerily similar to Zaina's. But there's an emptiness in her gaze that no amount of alchemy can hide, a trace of resistance in the way she inclines her head.

"Your Majesty." Whatever lingering, unreasonable doubts I have held that Madame and Ulla are one and the same effectively dissipate the moment she speaks.

The accent is different, posher and more refined, but her voice is the same as it was the first time I heard her laughing at the winter festival. I think about that now, the way she was so captivating. Intriguing. Unlike anything I'd ever seen.

Did she poison me then, too, dose me with something to convince me I was in love with her? Or was I truly so naïve?

It's impossible to imagine feeling anything amorous for her now.

"Lady Delmara." There is no trace of the ire I feel in

my carefully controlled tone. "Thank you for seeing me on such short notice."

"Of course. I hope you'll forgive the unusual circumstances." She gestures around the room with a self-deprecating expression. "I find I'm not much up to company these days, and I imagined you would prefer privacy for this conversation."

Her golden eyes leave me to land on Khijhana instead, but she doesn't say a word about her.

And why would she? According to Zaina, even the chalyx doesn't pose a threat to Ulla's impenetrable skin.

After a breath, she reaches her hand out for me to take. Forcing a foot forward, I take it, though my skin crawls with every point of contact.

"Do sit down. We are family, after all..." Her tone is clipped as she pauses for me to supply the name she is allowed to call me.

"Please, call me Einar," I respond, taking my seat across from her.

She sits with unnatural stillness for a moment, until she leans forward to take a steaming cup from the table. It strikes me that she is not hiding her true nature as well as I would expect, as well as she has in the past.

If I didn't know better, I might even think she was nervous.

Which means it's more important than ever to convince her that I am nothing more than a grieving widower.

"I would be honored," she says, the practiced sincerity in her tone almost believable. Her eyes land on my untouched teacup with a touch too much interest. "I hope you like chamomile."

Maybe she wouldn't risk killing me by poison when I

made a very public affair of coming to see her today, but a truth serum could prove to be just as deadly.

"I find that I can't stomach tea these days."

"Of course. My apologies." She waves a hand like it doesn't matter, but the gesture is strained. "You said you had a matter to discuss with me?"

"Yes. I wanted to come here today to give you my condolences. Your niece was—" I nearly choke on the lie until I will myself to focus on how close Zaina came to actually dying, willing it to show on my features. "She was one of the best things that has ever happened to me, and I am sorry for your loss."

I wasn't prepared to admit that freely, so I pause, allowing her to digest my words. She swallows, and I would almost believe there was real grief in her expression if I didn't know her to be a monster.

"But, I also came to tell you the truth about her death," I add.

In a nearly imperceptible movement, Ulla's head tilts to the side, her eyes narrowing before she smooths her expression. I'm not sure if she's assessing me for honesty, or if this news is genuinely shocking to her.

"Why would you lie about such a thing?" She makes a show of sinking back into her chair, the barest tremble of fear in her tone. "Was it this beast? Was it you?"

Khijhana growls, and I put a placating hand on her head.

"Of course not," I reply, not bothering to keep the offense from my voice. "The chalyx was her... pet. And I would never have hurt her."

"Then how did she die?" Ulla's affected accent is clipped and laced with something deadly.

"It was a dragon that killed her," I offer flatly, since she already knows as much from Dvain, but I don't miss the way her eyes light up when she hears it confirmed. "I was devastated when I woke up in the middle of the night to find her gone. I still cannot make sense of what she was doing riding that far from home, or how she wound up in that cave."

It isn't difficult to inject my tone with despair, remembering the way I found her that night.

Ulla blinks slowly, her breaths rising and falling in quick succession. She makes a show of disbelief. "And yet, you let the world believe her death was an accident."

"My people believe deeply in the lore about the dragon, that it only kills those who are unworthy of life," I say quietly. "I didn't want them to remember Zaina that way."

"I see." Ulla is lost in her own thoughts for several beats. "Have you heard from our friend Dvain?"

Not since Zaina strangled him to death.

It isn't good that she's already noticing his absence, though. Hopefully she'll assume he's been diverted.

"Not since I left home, no."

"I hope tragedy did not befall him as well."

I wouldn't call it a tragedy.

I open my mouth to respond when Ulla cuts me off, abruptly getting to her feet.

"Apologies, Your Highness, but I'm afraid I need to rest now after such an emotionally taxing visit." Her voice is tinged with the slightest bit of nervous energy as she quickly moves her hands behind her back.

Khijhana growls, but Ulla ignores her.

"Of course, Lady Delmara. Thank you for seeing me today."

"The servants will see you out." She gives a bare curtsy,

then spins to leave. She hasn't quite shut the door behind her when the coloring in her neck mottles, vacillating from her current light bronze back to the deeper brown she used to have.

The alchemical tonic she used clearly didn't last as long as she hoped for. I resist the urge to smirk.

Whatever she wants the world to believe, the woman has weaknesses, and I plan to find a way to exploit every single one of them.

CHAPTER TWENTY-FIVE

AIKA

I was suspicious when Mother sent me on a needless errand this morning, so I made every effort to hurry back. I had returned home in time to eavesdrop on the tail end of a conversation between her and the Jokithan King, but it had only left me feeling more confused.

So I find myself looking for an opportunity to sneak into his carriage. The guard who drove him here is vigilant, but he doesn't know the grounds like I do, and I doubt he's looking for someone as small as I am. I hide behind a couple of well placed bushes before easing my way into the vehicle.

King Einar's carriage is predictably spacious, though that won't be enough room to save myself if the giant cat decides to make me its dinner.

It's a chance I'm willing to take.

In a way, I was right when I accused him of coming to pretend to grieve, even if some of it didn't sound entirely fake. But the story about the dragon... What could he possibly have to gain by telling Mother that?

Was it truly just to assuage his conscience? His guilt, because he was the one who drove her out there?

My heartbeat thunders in my ears for reasons I can't entirely pin down, but I do know that for someone who has spent their entire life lying to people, I suddenly care a whole hell of a lot about the truth.

The front door to the estate slams shut, so I press myself into the darkness near the drawn curtains on the other side, hoping to at least avoid notice initially.

When the carriage door swings open, of course, *of sands-blasted course,* the cat gets in first. It growls, but Einar is right on its heels.

If I'm expecting to catch the king off guard, I am somewhat disappointed. His eyes widen when he notices me, and his hand goes out to soothe the cat, but he wordlessly clambers the rest of the way into the carriage.

Only when we're sitting across the space from one another with the tiger-like creature in between, does one of us decide to speak.

"Not going to let your tiger take a bite out of me, then?" The carriage lurches into motion, punctuating my words with the sound of clacking wheels.

"Khijhana doesn't appear to have any interest in eating you," the king responds in an even tone.

Khijhana. I can't help the small, bitter laugh that escapes me, mingling with my anger. The cat was Zaina's then. Or at least, she named it.

"She must not have liked it very much," I say, mostly because I suspect he gave it to her.

He furrows his brow, and I expound.

"Khijhana. It means something like small, annoying thing."

Rather than taking offense, the king lets out a

surprised bark of laughter. "I guess *Khijhana* grew on her, then."

Fury courses through me. How dare he take my sister, push her into death, lie about it, then try to share some kind of nostalgic moment with me.

He assesses me for a moment, like he senses my shift in mood despite the casual facade I am putting on. "Aika, I presume?"

I narrow my eyes before nodding. "What gave it away?"

I can only imagine what Mother might have said to him about me, especially in comparison to my beautiful, accomplished... dead sister. I suck in a breath, trying to find the numbness I seek at times like these, times when the memories won't stop.

"The rage did," Einar says softly.

I look up at him sharply.

"She said once that you had an endless supply of passion, for everything you did. Passion, though, can so easily be translated to anger"

"She said that?" The question pops out in spite of myself. I didn't expect Zaina to have talked about me at all, least of all to him.

He nods, and I swallow back a wave of emotion.

"You talk about her fondly, for someone who knew her scarcely three months and branded her a whore for the world to see."

"Would you rather I speak badly of her?" He sounds genuinely curious, if a bit exasperated.

"I'd rather you didn't speak of her at all," I snap. "Unless you'd like to tell me what drove my brilliant cousin to feel that her best option was absconding in the freezing night, chancing the frigid temperatures in an unknown land rather than go back to whatever life the two of you had together."

Something like pain flits through his gaze, but I'm not sure I believe it. I'm not sure I even want to. So instead, I drive the knife in deeper.

"What was she doing, far enough from you that it took you several hours to catch up to her? Was she trying to get away from you?"

"I don't know." His features are neutral, but I can practically smell the lie.

"Really? Then tell me, what did you do to her that she would rather risk her life, alone, than tell you where she was going that night?"

For the first time, he looks affected by something I've said. Tension permeates the carriage like a dense, impenetrable fog.

"I won't pretend I was a good husband to her," Einar responds after several silent moments. His carefully blank face is almost enough to make me buy into the undercurrent of grief I sense there. Almost. "But I didn't hurt her, if that's what you're asking."

"Then why?" The words barely come out a whisper.

"I don't know why." His voice is gentle, and I hate it.

I want him to scream and rage and be the monster to me that he must have been to her.

"I'm sure I don't have to tell you that Zaina played her cards close to her chest."

No, he doesn't. Which begs the question, why did he?

I examine his features, turning over what he said in my mind. His icy blue eyes are sincere, but there is something in them that I can't bring myself to believe, not entirely. Perhaps he isn't lying, but he isn't quite telling the truth either.

It's a struggle, finding a way to ask him for more without revealing too much of my own. The carriage shifts, the wheels going from packed earth to cobblestone, and I bite back a curse.

Unless I want to explain my simple outfit and my presence in Einar's carriage to the entire castle, I'm out of time, and I haven't gotten any real answers yet.

"One last question," I ask him.

He nods warily.

"Did you love her?" I don't know why I bother to ask that, when three months is hardly enough time to love anyone.

To see if he'll lie about it? To see what it will look like when he does?

Einar freezes. Whatever he had been expecting me to ask, I get the feeling I have finally caught him completely off guard. He sucks in a breath like he's about to answer, then lets it out in a whoosh of air.

When he's deliberated too long, and I'm well and truly out of time, I scoff.

"That's what I thought. Then don't pretend to grieve her, *Your Majesty.*" I open the carriage door, preparing to hop out.

"Wait," he says, and I turn expectantly. "My relationship with Zaina is--*was*... complicated. *She* was complicated." He massages the bridge of his nose, his eyes going distant.

"I don't even know why I asked," I mutter. "Obviously you didn't, but it's not like she loved you, either. Love really doesn't factor into our lives."

"That isn't true," he says sharply, and for a moment I think he's offended that I said she didn't love him. But he looks at me earnestly. "Regardless of how she felt about me, I know that she loved the girls she called her sisters. More than she loved herself." There's real emotion in his voice now, and I'm not sure how to take it. "She would have done anything for you."

Anything except come back to us.

Abruptly, I realize there is nowhere in the world I want to be less than in this carriage with this man who I'm beginning to suspect actually did care for my sister.

I am so desperate to get away from the accusations and regret invading every inch of this space, I don't even bother to respond to him. I peek out the window, waiting for the bushes I know are near the castle gates before slipping out of the carriage and shutting the door behind me.

If I'm right about what happened, and if the king isn't to blame for her taking her own life, then who or what is?

The years we spent together should have been enough time for me to understand her. I was just too busy competing with her to pay attention.

Now she's dead. She folded her hand, but I'm the one who lost.

CHAPTER TWENTY-SIX

AIKA

*W*hen I arrive back at the estate, Mother is in her bedroom and the servants are nowhere to be found.

I let myself in, slipping the door shut behind me. It's clear why she has ordered the servants away. She doesn't like anyone to know she can change her appearance at will.

Wearing wigs is one thing, and she puts the drops in her eyes that keep them looking golden brown more often than not, but the tonic is an ace she likes to keep up her sleeve.

Here she sits, in the middle of the day in her most public home, her skin mottling between umber and bronze while her obsidian fingernails clack against the gilded armrests in an agitated pattern.

"I've done as you asked, Mother," I announce, pretending not to notice the way her nerves are clearly on edge.

Because of King Einar? Is all of this because of his visit?

"And?" she demands. "What did you find out about Einar's purpose in being here?"

Again, I hear the odd note of familiarity when she says his name.

My mind whirls, trying to put the pieces together, all the things that are intricately tied to my sister's death. The irony is that if Zaina were here, she probably would have figured this out by now.

But if Zaina were here, none of this would be happening.

I inhale a sharp breath, shielding against the sudden onslaught of pain and trying to remember what Mother just asked me.

"Nothing," I say belatedly. "Other than everyone talking about the tiger, it's only rumors, nothing that even made sense."

Nothing makes sense.

"Chalyx," she corrects absentmindedly. Instead of questioning me further like she normally would, she only waves me away. "Leave it be for now. You have bigger things to worry about, anyway."

Like marrying into the biggest country this side of the world, which only causes more questions to churn in my mind.

I practically flee from the room before she can see the mutinous ideas that have been forming in my head since the day Damian brought news of Zaina's death.

Corentin is bigger than Jokith, with more trade routes and more influence. If she planned on one of us marrying here anyway, why send Zaina, who she constantly referred to as her most valuable asset, to Jokith first?

It doesn't make sense, unless there was something

specific there that she wanted, something more than just power.

For the first time in as long as I can remember, I allow myself to wonder what the point is of Mother's endless machinations.

And if they were worth Zaina dying for.

*S*hadows dance along my bedroom wall for hours, the reflection of the firelight taunting me with depictions of the nightmares I have been failing to keep at bay.

I close my eyes to avoid them and am faced instead with questions that have no answers playing on an endless loop in my mind.

The longer I lay here, the more I convince myself I am devolving into madness.

Hours pass, or minutes, I'm not sure which, but it's long enough that my skin begins to crawl, like something is trying to slowly claw its way out of my body.

Long enough to know that if I don't get out of this room, don't *do* something with all of this pent-up insanity, I'm going to implode.

Without thinking about the consequences, I slip out my small window and shimmy down to the ground, easily evading Mother's guards.

They weren't trained as I was. Their skills aren't forged in blood.

The moon is gone tonight, and I can't help but feel as if even that small bit of light has abandoned me. There is nothing but darkness now, everywhere I look.

I roam the streets for hours, trying to get my conversation with Einar out of my head.

Trying to ignore the way that hope had surged in my chest for the smallest fraction of a moment when I smelled Zaina in his rooms, replaced by a soul crushing emptiness when I beheld the very real grief on the king's features.

She's gone.

My sister is gone, and she's never coming back.

I hear her throaty laugh and see her flip her midnight waves and feel the way her hand would clench around mine in warning when Mother came storming through in a mood.

I see the way she would angle herself in front of me, edging me out of Mother's vision, and I would stupidly think it was because she wanted the attention for herself.

I didn't see that she was protecting me, and now that I do, I'll never have the chance to tell her that I understand.

My skin crawls even more, like it can't contain the maelstrom building within me.

All around me, inside me, is darkness.

So I go to create a light of my own.

🔥

My feet carry me to a rundown warehouse on the outskirts of the slums.

It's a base for drug pushers who have taken to dallying in slavery lately.

Two birds. One stone.

Raw energy courses through my veins, propelling my every move. I circle around the back and slip in through an open window without even bothering to glance inside, stepping behind the closest man and neatly cutting his throat.

He falls to the floor with a soft thud, and I step over his bleeding corpse, daring the others in the room to make their move.

Most of them are seated around a table, smoking cigars, while a few stand toward the perimeter. It doesn't take them long to notice me.

Once their initial shock wears off, shouts of alarm ring out and everything erupts into chaos.

How do you know he didn't have a family? Remy's voice melds with Zaina's in a twisted harmony in my head, but I ignore them both.

If these men have family, those families are better off without them. No one who does the things these men do should live.

I allow that thought to drive me as all nine of the remaining men charge toward me.

My mind races through all of the possibilities of how this fight will go. Who will make what move, and what are the odds I have of making it out of here alive?

I'm betting on the house tonight, and I'm all in.

With lightning-fast movements, I pull out my throwing stars and hurl them toward two of the men, killing each of them in a single blow.

Maybe they were forced into this, Zai's voice insists. *Maybe they had no choice.*

But everyone has a choice. I made mine, and maybe someday I will pay for it just as these men are now.

A knife comes flying my way, and I duck away from its

trajectory before snatching the hilt out of the air. Then I spin around and plunge it into the gut of the man trying to sneak up behind me. His blood sprays on my face, coating my vision crimson.

All I see is blood. It seeps its way into my soul and stains every last inch of me.

Six to go.

One tries to flee out the back door, and I fling another of my stars.

Make that five.

I tell myself the world is better off without them. They're terrible people.

Is anyone really all bad?

"Shut up, Zai!" I yell the words out loud, and the men surrounding me pause.

Stupid of them, because I use that distraction to aim a kick at one's groin while throwing a fourth star at one to my left. They both go down, though only one of them is still breathing.

Time slows as I lift my dagger to end his life. My breaths are coming too quickly again, and I try to pace them with the steps of the four hulking men closing in on me.

Am I turning into Damian?

The thought makes me stumble.

Maybe I'm there already. I shake my head and blink my eyes. No. I'm not as bad as he is, taking innocent victims at random. At least these men deserved to die.

Do you really think you get to make that judgment? This time, it's only Remy's voice condemning me.

Yes, I answer.

This justice is all I know. It's the only way to balance out the scales of all the things I've done.

I carry that thought with me, allowing it to fuel me on.

One of the men swings a blade to my left and I dodge away from it, just not quickly enough. The steel scrapes across my thigh. It stings like hell, but at least it isn't deep enough to do any real damage.

With my other leg, I land a kick on the man's jaw, sending him flying backward. He hits the corner of the table with a loud crack before falling to the ground.

He doesn't get up again.

My heartbeat roars in my ears, making it nearly impossible to hear anything else. Not the breaking of glass when one man shatters a bottle of whiskey on the edge of a chair before he hurls it at me. Not the furious screams of the man with the red face, charging toward me. Not the curses forming on the lips of the third and final man left standing.

And certainly not the sound of my blade as it slices neatly through each one of their guts.

It takes me several breaths to realize there is no one left standing to fight. The roaring in my ears shifts into a ringing until I can make out the sounds of a man groaning in pain behind me.

Slowly, I turn around to face him, but he's lying on the ground, clinging to his groin. I don't hesitate before I throw my blood-stained dagger at him, effectively cutting off the noise.

Nausea crashes over me like the waves of the ocean on a stormy night. Whether it's for the blood I've spilled or the realization that I could do this every night for the rest of my life and it still wouldn't matter, I'm not sure.

I have just enough humanity left to drip the bottle of fluid that keeps the fire from spreading in a circle around the edges of the wall.

Then, I douse the building and light the bloody thing on fire.

That's one good thing about the drug houses, at least. With all those chemicals, they're quick to go up in flames.

CHAPTER TWENTY-EIGHT
AIKA

The freezing night air is sobering, which is worse than whatever I felt inside the building. It seeps into me, chilling me to the bone and making me acutely aware of each speck of blood on my skin.

The world around me spins as I pace the cobblestone street.

My face is wet.

From the snow?

From tears?

From blood?

The flames soar higher in the air, and the numbness I felt in the warehouse abandons me entirely.

My chest hurts.

I can't breathe.

Raising a fist, I slam it against my breastbone again and again, trying to stop the pain.

I'm worried I'll have to miss you, too. Mel's voice is the next to torment me this evening, carving into me like a jagged knife to my rib cage.

Was she right?

Of course, she was.

If I keep going this way, I'll... I'll end up dead. Just like—

I hit my chest again, this time in an attempt to make my heart stop hurting.

She's dead.

Echoes from the night we learned about Zaina's death come ebbing back in, threatening to suffocate me.

A scream escapes my lungs, and I stare up at the stars, cursing them for staying so still. For being so consistently unhelpful. Were these the same stars that Zaina saw the night she died? Did they watch her burn? Did they care?

I light another match and throw it at the already burning building in front of me.

I need more.

More heat. More flames. More... *something.*

Grabbing the last bottle of accelerant from my bag, I hurl it toward the building and watch as more flames burst and break free from the warehouse. They fly toward the street, the sky, anywhere they can to escape, angry and wild and reckless.

Like me, I think and begin to laugh, a tortured sound, followed by another scream.

I'm pacing again, shaking my head and cursing everyone and everything around me. How? How did it come to this?

"You left me!" I cry aloud, stumbling back from another outburst of flames and glass.

"You left me to become... *this!*" My voice breaks on the words.

Zaina had always kept me from falling, from diving in too deep and drowning in the waves of the chaos in our lives. But now?

I take a shuddering breath, willing my lungs to stop punishing me.

Now, I'm burning men alive, and not for Mother. I intentionally added even more red to my ledger of death for little more reason than a whim.

At least, there were only ten this time.

Only ten...

I scoff.

When did I become this person? A person who feels better when her nightly death count is lower than the one before?

And this time, instead of killing them for the crimes they committed, this time it was Einar and my mother, and Damian, and even a sands-blasted dragon that I was slaying. Anyone, everyone, who had a hand in taking Zaina to that frozen place.

To her death.

More liquid streams down my face, and I can't seem to care if it's tears or blood. Maybe it's better that it's blood, that this is all coming to an end soon.

A small, weak sound comes from me, and I hate myself for it.

I couldn't save her. I couldn't save Zaina, or Jessa, or any damned person worth saving.

A sob escapes me, and I fall to my knees, ignoring the way the stones cut into my skin.

Logically, I know it's only been a couple of minutes since I left the burning building. Logically, I know I need to run, to get as far away from here as possible, before the guards find me. Before Damian does...

But I can't move. My head is in my hands, and I'm rocking back and forth, pounding my fists against my skull.

I'm desperate. Desperate to feel something else, something other than the pain inside. Desperate to make it stop.

Maybe Damian will come just in time for the two of us to die in the fire. Maybe I'll get to watch as he's engulfed in flames just before I am. I can die the same way that Zaina did, watching our dear *brother* burn.

There are worse ways to go.

I rock back and forth again, unable to drown out all of their voices. They blend together in my mind, an orchestra of judgment and taunting. I slam my fist against my head again, trying to quiet them. Trying to rid myself of each of their faces.

Everyone I couldn't save, and everyone I murdered.

It's too much.

Another blow to my temple leads to another and another in my failed attempts to drown out the cacophony in my head.

Finally, one voice rings out louder than all the rest, and somehow, even after everything, it's the one that cuts the deepest.

CHAPTER TWENTY-NINE
ZAINA

*I*t takes me hours to find Aika.

I can't explain what sent me after her, except that Einar's description of her in the carriage had alarm bells going off in my head, had me wondering what she might do to herself.

What she might do to anyone in her path.

At least, I am inconspicuous in the traditional headpiece that leaves only my eyes uncovered. Easterners are common enough here that I won't stand out, and no one can see my face.

Small mercies, when everything is going to hell.

When the cloying smell of smoke hits me, I let loose a string of curses. As I race toward the source a few buildings away, I can practically hear a much younger Aika's voice in my head.

"That's why they call me The Flame," she says, *a smug grin on her face when I finally pull my hand away from the fire.*

It's only one of Madame's many daily training exercises, seeing who can withstand pain the longest.

"No one calls you that." I scowl.

"You clearly need more practice." Madame shakes her head in disappointment, and I know it will mean the dungeons for extra training.

My hand wasn't hurting yet, but better me than Aika. At least I'm used to the things Madame puts me through in the dungeons.

I turn back only to see Aika testing her hand over the fire again, ready to see if she can beat her time from before.

I squeeze my eyes shut in consternation.

Keeping her safe is a lost cause, but it's not one I can make myself give up just yet.

Damn it.

I knew.

I knew the second I read that stupid story that it sounded just like something she would do, but I convinced myself I was wrong because she's never gone against Madame.

She lives for an adrenaline rush, though, and she never, *ever* knows when to say "when."

The vigilante. She's going to get herself killed. Or worse.

Is this because Madame told her she had to marry the prince? At least, I assume she knows, with the masquerade only two days away.

I stumble down the alleyway just in time to hear her voice cry out.

"You left me!" she yells.

I freeze in my tracks, my very core going cold.

Einar said she was grieving, but I didn't quite believe it. Aika doesn't grieve. She doesn't wallow. She forges ahead, unburdened by the ugliness around us.

At least, I thought she did.

I force myself forward to peer around the corner.

"You left me to become... this." She barely gets the last word out, her fists clenching.

The words echo down to the hollowest part of my soul, piercing the deepest, rawest parts of me.

It was me. I did this to her.

The weight of her anger and grief washes over me as if it's my heart she is squeezing in her hands. The building is in flames, but instead of running away, she stares at the fire ahead.

What have I done?

I wanted to protect them. It never occurred to me that I might break them in the process.

It never occurred to me that Aika was breakable at all. At least... not like this.

She pounds her fist against the side of her head, and I am done. This has gone on long enough. Whether I can trust her or I can't, I will pitch my fate alongside hers to save her from another moment of this suffering.

I move to step out of the alleyway when a dark shape emerges from the other side of the building. A man.

No.

My dagger is already in my hand, and I am prepared to hurl it directly into the man's throat when I catch sight of his features in the wan moonlight.

What in the bloody hell is he doing here?

CHAPTER THIRTY
AIKA

"Gemma?" Remy's voice sounds like it's coming from under water.

But I'm so tired. I'm not sure I can stand up against the weight of his judgment anymore, especially not after tonight.

"Gemma." He calls to me again, and this time it's a little clearer.

I realize he's standing in front of me, looming over me from his substantial height. His mouth forms the name "Gemma" once more, his eyes flooded with something I can't decipher.

I shake my head, another denial he can't possibly understand.

No, I want to scream. *Aika. Not Gemma. Not The Flame. Not the vigilante.*

But those wouldn't be true either. Nothing feels true anymore.

Turning to face him, I hold out my bloody wrists and sliced-up hands. I hadn't been nearly as careful to protect them tonight, and I'm certain the red coating them is nearly as much my blood as that of the dead men.

Flames blaze in Remy's eyes, the light of the fire dancing across his face in a pattern that's almost mesmerizing.

He doesn't speak, though.

His gaze darts behind me before he closes the distance between us, crouching in front of me.

A warm weight settles over my shoulders, and only then do I realize I am shivering. It's his cloak. Without a word, he scoops me into his arms. I don't protest.

As always, he smells like sage and lavender, making me painfully conscious that all I smell like is ashes and death.

"Coming to haul me away to the magistrate?" I rasp out.

"No." He says the word like a curse.

"I knew you were bluffing."

A bitter huff of air escapes him, but he doesn't respond. It might be the first time I've seen him at a loss of words, but then, it's the first time he's found me in a broken heap outside a burning building full of roasting bodies, so I guess it's a night of firsts.

Suddenly, that strikes me as funny.

I let out a giggle that morphs into a sob, and he only shakes his head. I don't expect him to understand the way that anything can be funny in the right circumstances... or the wrong ones.

After all, he's a far cry from street-rat orphan turned mass murderer turned soon-to-be princess.

We don't speak anymore, and he eventually puts me down. He grips my wrist, though, like he's afraid I'll disappear if he doesn't keep hold of me. He tugs me all the way to the back entrance of the Drunken Pumpkin, up to my cramped boarding room, and lights the lantern.

"I'll be right back," he says. "Don't go anywhere... or set anything on fire." A ghost of a smirk breaks through his troubled expression, and it occurs to me that he's handling me with kid gloves.

I don't think that I mind that right now.

I settle onto my bed, not sure staying is a good idea but having no real desire to leave, either. The door creaks open only minutes later, revealing Remy with a basin of water and a clean cloth.

He crosses over to me, kneeling in front of me before dipping the cloth in the water. Then he raises the cloth to my cheek, slowly wiping at the blood I know has gathered there.

His hands are strong, calloused from the weapons he trains with. I've felt their strength, seen their grace, and even experienced their skill firsthand.

But this tenderness is something new.

Neither of us speaks or tries to joke as he gently cleans the blood from my face and my hands. I want to tell him that the blood on my hands can't be washed away as easily as this, that there are some stains that can never come out, and that my soul itself runs crimson now.

I don't, though, because I suspect he already knows.

He carefully wraps the wound around my leg, his fingers grazing the inside of my thigh and igniting me with a different kind of heat than the subtle burn of my scrapes and bruises.

Still, I don't say anything at all until he winces when he gets to the cuts on my knuckles.

"Sympathy for the murderer?" I ask.

"I told you, mercy is not a finite resource." He inhales

like he might say something else, but silence reigns once more.

"Mercy," I barely breathe out the word, but it is still loud in the quiet space. I look from the fingers that are more holding my hands than cleaning them, to the turmoil in his deep brown eyes, the slight parting of lips that are suddenly so, so close to mine. "Is that all this is?"

"Gem—"

I move forward, my mouth pressing against his and cutting off the deception he was on the verge of unwittingly uttering. I can't handle any more lies right now.

Or any more truths, for that matter.

But his lips soften against mine and I know that this, us... It's neither lie nor truth, neither right nor wrong.

It exists on a plane separate from all of those things. It exists in this moment, in the feeling of his lips skating from mine down to my jaw, his fingers clenching around my thighs.

And I need more of it.

I lean into him fully, arching my back so his mouth can travel to my neck, my collarbone, and lower. Quick fingers untie the laces of my outer corset, deftly removing every confining inch of fabric between us.

He brings his mouth back up to mine, a low growl emanating from him when I dart my tongue out to taste him. The hands that were so tender before grip my hips firmly, pulling me against him.

My skin is unnaturally hot, like the fire itself still rages within me, while Remy is cooler, more solid.

We are on opposite sides of every battlefield imaginable, but right now, it feels like the melding of his skin against mine is the only thing that grounds me, the only thing that makes me feel real.

At least, until he stops.

I feel the moment he breaks our contact, backing away slowly. The laces of his shirt are open, and I fix my gaze on the several exposed inches of defined chest.

"Gemma." His voice is soft, like he's still afraid I might break if he speaks too loudly.

I don't blame him. I feel that way, too.

"We can't," he says. "We shouldn't do this again. Not tonight. Not when..." He trails off, piercing me with a probing stare. "What happened to you, Gemma? The fires, the slavers... is this about your friend? Did the slavers take her, too?"

I close my eyes, shaking my head against an onslaught of memories. "I don't want to talk about her. I don't want to talk about anything."

"You never do." He sighs, and there's a deep sadness in the sound.

I still haven't opened my eyes when I hear the sound of him getting to his feet. My hand darts out of its own accord, closing around his wrist.

"Stay." The word is out before I can stop it.

I can't remember ever asking anyone to stay when they wanted to leave. Not my father, who abandoned me when the responsibilities of parenting became too much. Not my sister, when I felt her slipping away.

Sure as hell not any man.

I pull my shirt back onto my shoulder from where it's fallen askew, covering myself so he doesn't think that's what I'm asking for. I open my eyes and raise them to Remy's, letting him see how much I need this.

How much I need *him*.

"Why? When we both know how this ends?" The words come out a whisper.

Because I feel like I might cease to exist without you here to ground me right now. Because when you're around, I almost feel like a person instead of a weapon, molded and honed into something sharp and deadly by the cruelest person I know.

I can't seem to make myself come up with a reason that makes sense, even in my own head, so I just give him a small, rare bit of truth.

"Because everything ends, one way or another. But it doesn't have to end like this."

His head shakes, the barest fraction of an inch. I'm sure he's going to walk away when he surprises me by sitting down next to me instead.

"All right. I'll stay."

CHAPTER THIRTY-ONE

AIKA

$\mathcal{T}$he bed grows colder by the second.

My sleep is more fitful without Remy here to chase my nightmares away. I shiver and wrap the threadbare blanket tighter around myself, but it doesn't help. Frost nips at the small window of the room and a fog forms with each of my breaths.

But it isn't just the temperature that chills me. It's the distinct lack of *him.*

When I finally leave the bed, I take a quick glance around the room.

No note.

I fight back the memories of the random notes he used to write whenever he had to leave unexpectedly, the little gestures and messages that gave away bits and pieces of him. How he had made it clear that he cared, and how I had pretended not to.

It's plain to see in hindsight that I left the tavern that day without letting him explain the woman who had dragged him away because it was easier than confronting my feelings for him. Easier than giving into them and letting him become collateral damage of my life.

Though it seems that happened anyway.

My gut churns as I throw on one of the clean dresses I keep in the makeshift closet here.

Of course he left.

Maybe it really was just about mercy. Maybe that's all it's ever been about.

I am the epitome of everything he hates, and I suppose him leaving without a word is the gentlest goodbye he could offer.

A hollowness fills me once again, and every nerve ending in my body is raw and exposed. I go through the motions of tying the laces on my boots with limbs that feel too heavy.

My hands freeze when I catch sight of the bloodied cloths left on the chair. The memory of him gently tending to my wounds is still fresh and hurts more than the cuts and scrapes he cleaned and wrapped for me.

Grabbing my cloak from the rack on the wall, I toss it into the waste bin by the door. There is no sense bringing it with me. Not when it smells of smoke and Remy and so much death.

I snag the extra one I keep here and wrap it around my shoulders, throwing the hood over my head without even bothering to comb the knots from my hair.

I tell myself that it's better this way. Mother has plans for me that don't involve me being Gemma, or The Flame, and certainly not the vigilante anymore.

No more gambling halls. No more Remy. No more playing my fiddle in King's Square. And certainly, no more fires...

With a final glance around the room, I shut the door behind me, closing this chapter of my life for good.

CHAPTER THIRTY-TWO
AIKA

he sun hasn't quite risen yet, and I'm careful to sneak around the gates of the estate and into the bushes beneath my window. Once I know it's clear, I begin the arduous task of scaling the wall.

The motion tugs at the scrapes on my hand, but the promise of Mother's healing tonic in my room propels me upward. A few moments later, and I'm in without a sound.

I have just enough time to down the liquid, remove my bandages, hide them behind my pillow, and muss up the bed before my door bursts open.

Mother cocks her head to the side like a predator. "Have you gone deaf?"

With all the ease I can muster, I hide my still-healing hands behind my back and stuff down the fear that's beginning to creep up my spine. She told me to be more careful, and yet, here I am. Standing before her with my hands and leg still bleeding, waiting for the tonic to kick in before she notices.

"No, Mother." I force contrition into my voice.

"Then why did I have to call for you more than once?"

ELLE MADISON & ROBIN D. MAHLE

She continues without waiting for an answer. "Honestly, Aika. One useless daughter is quite enough."

I focus on the tingling of the tonic stitching my skin back together, not so much as twitching an eyebrow at her comment about Mel.

She isn't nearly angry enough to account for my being out all night. She isn't demanding explanations or throwing me in the dungeons.

Can it actually be that she doesn't know?

"Yes, of course. I apologize, Mother." I hide the relief I feel by turning to face the washbasin and dipping my tingling hands into the water.

I watch as the last bit of skin heals over without so much as a scar, not that it would matter when my hands are covered with the evidence of a rough childhood in the slums.

The cool water feels good enough on my skin that I splash it on my face as well, wiping away some of the grime that's settled there.

Mother doesn't acknowledge my words, only launches into the details of what our day will hold while I dry my skin with a plush towel.

A final fitting for my ball gowns, the torturous removal of nearly all of my body hair, and one last rundown to be sure we know everything there is to know about everyone who will be in attendance.

She shoves a piece of parchment into my hand. "Memorize this."

The cramped page is filled with names. Somehow, she's obtained a list of the guests, the servants, and even the guards.

Guards.

I urgently rescan the list, my eyes painstakingly raking

over each name, but his name isn't here. The sinking feeling crashing over me doesn't feel quite as much like relief as it should.

Which is ridiculous, because if Remy recognizes me, his moral compass will never allow me to marry the prince he's sworn to protect.

"Is there a problem?" Mother arches a perfectly shaped eyebrow.

I relax my features. There's no reason to suspect I'll run into a random city guard in my capacity as a royal.

"Sorry, I was just thinking about how I could possibly get close to the prince with all of the other ladies there. I'm trying to run through everything I know about him so that I can have the upper hand." *Lies.*

Her violet eyes narrow. "I've already told you, the queen and I have an arrangement, unless you doubt me." Her hand darts up to grab my face, her nails digging into my cheeks like talons. "Or is it I who should be doubting you?"

Tension stretches between us like a fiddle string wound too tightly, poised to snap at the first touch of the bow.

I can't shake my head in her iron grip, so I settle for forcing words out, though my jaw is clamped together. "Of course not, Mother."

"See that I have no reason to, then. I don't expect to explain myself again." She drops her hand and spins around, leaving me to collect myself on shaking legs.

After last night, I wasn't sure I could feel things like fear or relief anymore, so I am surprised when both wash over me in alternating waves. Taking a deep, steadying breath, I finish readying myself for the day she has laid out.

169

It feels strange to be stepping back into her plans so quickly, but I don't have much choice. I can't afford to upset her again.

Zaina might be gone, but Mel isn't.

I suddenly hate myself for never responding to her letter, because she's right. We're all we have now.

And I will do whatever I have to in order to keep her.

🔥

My mind is brimming with information by the time I lug myself up the marble stairs to bed. I'm nine steps in when the hairs stand on the back of my neck. I don't need to turn around to know that Damian is following me.

He studied my every word and movement during Mother's tutelage with a speculative gaze, and I've been waiting for him to approach me ever since.

I speak without glancing over my shoulder.

"Will you be accompanying me all the way to my chambers? I must say how grateful I am to have such a loyal, albeit rabid, dog to make sure I arrive there safely."

Damian's shadow draws closer, completely overtaking mine.

"You speak so freely for someone who is a traitor to the woman who has given her everything." His tone is neutral, but I swear I can detect a note of amusement.

My heartbeat picks up speed, and I start to see stars. *Has he found me out? Did he see me there last night? Did he see me with Remy?*

"I think you have confused me with yourself, *Brother*," I respond quickly before he can sense my panic. "What in the bloody hell could I have done that you could possibly deem traitorous?"

I round the next curve of the winding staircase, not daring to slow my pace.

His low chuckle sounds behind me, and I resist the urge to shiver.

"I would imagine setting fires to Mother's *friends* would fall into that category," he says, and I nearly trip over the next step.

"Right, because that would make sense." I roll my eyes with feigned confidence. "One of her daughters, single-handedly destroying the empire she helped to build? You're reaching, Damian."

I reach the landing at the top of the stairs and lift an arm to open the door when rough fingers grab hold of it in a bruising grip.

I raise my bored gaze to meet Damian's, not giving him an ounce of satisfaction by getting a response from me.

"This entire time, I knew something was off. But I know the truth now," he says, leaning down closer to me. "I know it was you, *Vigilante.*"

His words are like tendrils of ice creeping down my spine, but I can't let him see that. So, I glare right back at him with more indignation than I have a right to bear.

"First of all," I begin, looking at where his hand still has my arm in a firm hold, "you have three seconds to let go of me before I rid you of whatever pathetic manhood you claim to possess." I twist the dagger I'd pulled from a secret pocket of my dress a little more into his groin.

He loosens his hold but doesn't let go.

I push the blade even farther, feeling the give of the fabric on his trousers, and he lets his hand drop.

"And secondly, what possible reason could you have to think--"

Damian cuts my words off when he holds up a couple of tarnished, sooty throwing stars. *My throwing stars... that I left at the fire.*

I will my thumping heart to calm. A moment of weakness is all he needs to go to Mother.

"It's interesting, is it not, that I could have sworn I'd heard your voice last night, right outside of one of Mother's *hul gil* distributors."

"Obviously, the fire destroyed more than just your disgusting face, Damian. We both know I don't deal with the distributors anymore," I say flatly, but Damian continues on as if I haven't spoken.

"But I was patient. I waited until the embers were gone, until the guards' backs were turned before I went inside to investigate. I found these." He examines the weapons slowly. "How very coincidental. My *sister's* favorite weapons sticking out of several of the men.

"And of course, you tried to throw Mother off of your trail, *a vigilante who sets fires when your enforcer is known as The Flame.* Here I thought Zaina was the only clever one," he says, his eyes leaving the metal to stare at me.

I raise an incredulous brow and cross my arms.

"It wasn't me, Damian, but I am sure you had your fun trying to frame me. For all I know, you planted those there. And besides," I make a show of examining my throwing stars more closely. "These aren't even mine. Any fool could see that. Mine are five pronged, not six, like these." *Lie.* I'm going to need to replace every one that I have left just in case he wants to check.

Damian's features slacken just a fraction as he looks them over again.

I tsk. "I can see that going over well, what with you already being in the *doghouse* and all. Do let me know what Mother says," I mock before I turn around to open the door to my room.

His arrogance gives way to something more doubtful. I take advantage of his hesitation to close my door with all the confidence I can muster.

Like I'm not guilty of everything he's accusing me of.

Like I'm not at all terrified that he will take me up on my offer and go running to Mother with all of this.

Bile rises in my throat, and I rush over to the window, throwing it open. I gulp down the icy air, my head spinning in time with my stomach.

I have no way of knowing if he believed me, if I at least gave him enough pause to stay his hand.

Now, it's just a waiting game to see if I will live or die on the mountain of lies and sins of my own making.

"I want to tell Aika tomorrow night," I announce when Einar returns from dinner with the king.

I haven't stopped thinking about my sister since I trailed her and Remy to her room above the bar.

Einar massages the bridge of his nose, letting out a sigh. "I still don't think the fact that she's burning buildings full of people is evidence enough that we can trust her."

"Buildings full of people who work for Madame," I clarify, my hands tightening around my teacup.

"Or people who crossed her," he argues, setting his crown on the table before sitting on the chair adjacent to mine. "We don't know."

"You didn't see Aika at that fire." I shake my head. "That wasn't just a job for Madame. Besides, we agreed that arson isn't her style. It's too obvious."

"We made an assumption when we had no stake in this, and now you want to risk absolutely everything on a hunch." A muscle ticks in Einar's jaw, the only evidence of his frustration.

"Do you have a better plan?" I try and fail to keep sarcasm out of my tone.

"I'll talk to her tomorrow at the ball, drop a few hints and see how she reacts."

It isn't the worst idea, giving ourselves an extra day to be sure we're doing the right thing. It wouldn't be unreasonable at all, except…

"So, your plan is to, what, use your wealth of insight on a woman you've met exactly one time to gauge her reactions?"

His face darkens, because he knows where I'm going with this, but I forge ahead anyway.

"You don't know my sister, and you can't read her." My tone is insistent. "Sands, I *do* know her, and I can barely read her, but it's better than nothing."

"You are not going to the masquerade," he says flatly.

I bristle. "Your permission is neither sought nor required, Einar. Besides, what happened to, *I'm sure of you?*"

I echo his words from the night of my coronation when he told me he believed we could defeat Madame.

"I am sure of you," Einar growls, leaning forward in his seat. "But our entire line of play depends on you staying dead. If Ulla discovers you're alive, you're risking everything we're trying to do and everyone we're trying to protect."

"Even Madame won't be able to recognize me in a masquerade mask in a dimly lit ballroom with paint on my face." *Probably.* "I've been trained to do this, to stick to the shadows and remain unseen in a crowd. Aren't you the one always telling me she's only human?"

"And what if you're wrong?" he pushes, rising to his feet now. "What if she does recognize you?"

"We could drown ourselves in what-ifs."

Einar raises his eyebrows, as cognizant as I am of the way I've avoided answering his question. I try again.

"We need Aika on our side."

"I am aware of that, but have you forgotten you took an oath to protect all of Jokith? You can't do that if you're dead."

"I hardly think a ball is a life-or-death situation."

"Everything that involves Ulla is a life-or-death situation, and it's not like this would be the first time you hurled yourself head-first into danger. There's no spring to save you here, Zaina." He's barely gritting out his words through clenched teeth.

"Is that why you made me Queen?" I tilt my head in disbelief. "To stay my hand?"

His expression hardens and his jaw clenches several times before he responds.

"Of course not, but I certainly won't complain if it compels you to see past the handful of things you deign to consider important."

Fury floods my veins. "So I should, what, hide in this room until *you* decide it's time to act?"

"I'm just asking you to be smart about this and not go rushing into anything. We're here to play the long game."

"That was before the long game required standing by and watching my sister be forced into marriage with a complete stranger!" I yell.

His expression shutters, his jaw slackening.

When he finally speaks, it's in a deceptively quiet voice. "You say that like it's a fate worse than death."

Silence descends, heavy with the weight of everything we've said and all we haven't.

I won't take the words back. My marriage to Einar

might have turned out for the better, in the end, but he will never understand what it is to be *sold* to another person like a piece of property.

"When Madame sold Aika's virginity, I couldn't stop her, but I promised myself I would never let anything like that happen to her again," I say evenly.

"And what about your promise to me that we wouldn't take unnecessary risks?" he asks, and there is an edge to the question.

"Don't make me choose between being a sister and a queen."

Einar's voice is bitter when he responds. "Between being a sister and a wife, you mean."

He stalks away before either of us can say another word.

CHAPTER THIRTY-FOUR

AIKA

*T*his morning was quiet and filled with an eerie semblance of normalcy. Damian hasn't said anything more on the subject of my being the vigilante, and Mother hasn't acted any stranger than normal.

She's not the type to hold off on her *discipline* with us, so I have to imagine that she still doesn't know anything.

Maybe it will be fine.

I ignore the voice in my head that tells me this marriage is another shackle on my long chain leading back to Mother. She has owned me since the day we met.

At least with this role, my bedroom will have a better view.

As soon as the thought enters my mind, guilt crashes over me in waves. She has taken me in, given me a home, and I balk when she asks something of me in return.

My stomach churns as I glance around the room, trying to remind myself of all that she's given me. But when my eyes land on the large, fake family portrait above the hearth, there is nothing I can do to make that sinking feeling go away.

Will I always be trading one lie for another?

I run a hand through my hair and sigh.

Celestial Hells, it was better when I didn't care.

I pour myself a dram of whiskey and down it in one go before a knock sounds at my door.

"Come in," I call out just before three maids bustle into the room holding the obscene gown Mother has chosen for me tonight.

For someone who enjoys the shadows, this dress is an unwelcome foray into the bright light. The fabric itself is a deep crimson, but iridescent beads glimmer in various shades of orange and yellow, each of them resembling a spark... or a flame.

How fitting.

I suppress a sigh and strip off my robe while the girls begin my transformation. Though their lives here are better than that of the servants at the Chateau, they still have very bleak prospects ahead of them with Damian around.

So, when they giggle or titter or gossip about the ball tonight and the other ladies there, I let them.

Especially once I see what they've done to me.

My long black hair is down in loose curls, with the sides pulled tightly back and pinned. A cascade of curls falls down my spine, right between mechanical works of art that resemble wings.

My lips are a crimson slash, like a streak of blood on my otherwise pale face. Even my eyes have changed, Mother's drops turning my irises amber with flecks of red throughout. Copper dust and long, false lashes complete the transformation.

The last thing they pull out is a golden, bejeweled

mask, definitely not one of the ones Mother showed me before. It has high, tendrilled points like flaming horns, inlaid with rubies. The mask parts at my nose, a tendril coming down on either side to brush against my jawbone.

I am unrecognizable, even to me. A dragon, fiery and fierce.

The maids are pulling on a set of matching gloves when Mother's voice sounds from the doorway.

"Perfection," she says. "You are even better than I'd hoped for."

I tell myself I don't care about her praise, don't lean into it like the leaves of a dying plant stretching up to the sun, desperate for the warmth and life it promises.

Mother is as put together as ever, but certainly not prepared for a ball.

"You aren't going." I inject the smallest lilt into my voice, unwilling to outright question her tonight.

"I want all eyes on you tonight, child." The implication is that they wouldn't be in her presence.

Her smile is brittle, though, and I can't help but remember the way she changed her appearance for King Einar.

She couldn't very well show up at court with a different skin color, even if the tonic was more stable. Is she hiding from him?

Something in my face must give away the troubled nature of my thoughts, but she misinterprets it because she makes a tsking sound.

"Remember, my daughter, that there is no need to worry," she says, lifting my chin with her fingertip, her long obsidian nail gently scraping my neck. "As long as you make a reasonable show of being noteworthy and bonding with the prince, no one will have cause to raise any questions."

With that bit of encouragement, she ushers me out the door.

Time to go meet my future husband.

CHAPTER THIRTY-FIVE
AIKA

*J*t's oddly off-footing, being surrounded by people in masks. Between that, my fitted dress, and the fact that I am only carrying one weapon this evening, I can't seem to stop looking over my shoulder.

It doesn't help that people are staring.

I loosen my grip around the black fan tied at my wrist.

To onlookers, it's an ordinary fan that ladies use to keep themselves cool or subtly communicate with, but mine has two blades at the ends, mostly hidden within the fabric. Razor sharp edges line the top as well, carefully colored matte black to blend in with the fabric.

A crowded ballroom may not be the most dangerous room I've ever been in, but I won't go anywhere unarmed.

A solid hundred ladies stand in a circle in the over-sized ballroom, awaiting the arrival of Prince Francis. There isn't much to be discerned with the masks, but several have angular eyes like mine, and medium-toned skin.

Others have skin as dark as the night sky, and a few are pale enough to rival King Einar.

Then there are those with skin a shade of light bronze and caramel-colored eyes so much like Zaina's that I have to look away.

Still, in a sea of blue and purple peacocks or black felines and snowy owls, a fiery dragon is sure to draw attention.

Mother plays her games well.

The royal family sits at the head of the ballroom, all except for the prince.

I can't help but scan the room for Remy in the rows of guards on either side of the royal family, even though his name wasn't on the list. He isn't there, but Lawrence is, his features more relaxed than I've seen them in town.

"All hail Prince Francis," the crier announces, beating his staff on the ground.

I follow Lawrence's expectant gaze to the doorway just in time to see the prince saunter into the room.

Sands.

Mother has played her game even better than I suspected.

The man isn't pasty or portly, from what little I can see of his skin, but he is the only other person in this room wearing red.

His mask is an effigy of a burning comet falling through the sky, topaz and rubies swirling up to meet sapphires and amethysts. His tunic is dyed in a similar fashion, but red is the predominant hue.

A subtle glow emanates from the fabric, matching the rest of the royal family. He stands out in the dimly lit room as if he truly is a comet, heading straight for us. The circle of ladies opens for him, then closes again around him.

Most of them are giggling or whispering to one

another, and one near me even speculates that the mask is hiding pustules on his face.

It wouldn't matter to me, but judging from his taut body and the confident way he carries himself, I have a feeling whatever is beneath the mask won't be too terrible to look at.

Francis walks in a slow circle, inspecting each of us like he's surveying contenders at the local festival. I barely suppress an eye roll, especially when I know it's all for show.

He has a gracious smile for each courtier who curtsies before him. Until me.

When his unnaturally green eyes meet mine, the corner of his mouth turns up in an arrogant smirk.

Do I amuse him?

I raise my chin higher, sweeping into a demure curtsy that makes me want to set myself on fire.

He makes a show of completing another circle before stopping again in front of me, sketching a flourished bow that's low to the point of mocking.

At least one of us is enjoying themselves.

"Would you honor me with this first dance?" he asks in the clipped accent of the upper class.

Disappointed sighs ring out from the ladies around us.

"The honor is mine." My accent mirrors his, my voice pitched lighter than usual with the breezy tone of a courtier.

I don't even choke on the sickly-sweet words.

He takes my hand. I can't help but notice that his is pleasantly warm, rougher than expected, and that it fits perfectly around my much smaller one. Tension crackles between us, even as his features remain poised in arrogance.

He pulls me onto the dance floor, but I wait to speak until a few other couples have joined us.

"It truly was an honor to be chosen." I try to feel him out, see what he knows of our arrangement.

"How could I resist, when we were matching so perfectly. And so coincidentally." His expression doesn't so much as twitch to betray his emotion.

His bright emerald eyes only stare indifferently over my head as he moves into the basic steps of this dance, waiting to see if I'll follow his lead.

Two can play at that game.

"Indeed," I say noncommittally, careful not to let a trace of sarcasm seep through. "What more could you possibly need in a bride?"

His gaze flies to my face, like he's trying to decipher the meaning behind my words, and I offer him a bland smile.

"Indeed," he murmurs.

A strange energy thrums between us, and I wonder if it is only the knowledge of what we will be to each other creating the odd tension. Despite his blatant attempts at nonchalance, he keeps stealing glances down at me, his speculative frown telling me he feels it, too.

Whatever *it* is.

He sighs, and it needles at me.

"Is the prospect of finding a wife really so boring for you?" I ask through the grin plastered on my face.

A low rumble goes through his chest, but there is no humor in it.

"Finding implies searching, both of which imply a choice I don't have." That answers the question of whether he knows about whatever Mother has set in motion, at least.

"Then I suppose that puts you on even footing with each of your prospects here," I say sharply. "Are you really so sad to be deprived of the chance to choose your bride from a three-day masquerade? Hmm." I make a show of thinking. "With our faces covered and so little time for conversing, I wonder whatever assets you could be taking into consideration."

Interest glints in his eye, and he finally looks at me full on.

"Historically, the purpose of the masquerade was to put the ladies of differing circumstances and influence on equal footing, but these days it's not as though there's any real mystery. To answer your question, though, no. I'm not particularly bothered by any *arrangements* that were made. One courtier is pretty much like the next, I suppose." His tone is light, dismissive, as though he honestly couldn't care less.

My lips part in offense. *Arrogant tosser.* If I weren't here to marry him, I would pull out my fan and show him just how *like the next courtier* I am. Before I can formulate a response, though, a commotion catches my attention from across the room.

The Jokithan King has arrived.

At least, I assume it's him, since I haven't seen any other hulking men with silver-blond hair and a giant chalyx in tow. He wears a silver wolf's mask, as brutal as it is beautiful, and a matching brocaded tunic with a high collar. Pale blue eyes survey the room, either failing to notice or deliberately ignoring the women already fawning over him.

Fury rises up in my chest. My sister is not yet cold in her grave. What is he even doing here, at a party? Is it politeness, or did I read him wrong?

Perhaps he is looking to replace her already.

Francis gives me a conspiratorial wink. "But perhaps you're bothered by it. What do you say, Lady Aika? Want to abandon your lowly dreams of marriage to a prince in favor of the king?"

Celestial Hells. I almost wish he were pasty and portly, at this point, rather than condescending and thoughtless. I glare at him until he looks me in the eye, rage overtaking any vestiges of propriety I have left.

"Would I care to marry my s — cousin's widower, you mean?" I catch myself before I say *sister*. "A mere month after her death?" My voice is sharper than the edges of the knives in the fan at my wrist.

He squeezes his eyes shut, chagrin pinching his features and replacing the mocking lilt to his voice. "I'm sorry. I didn't think—"

His earnest tone sounds different from the accented one he used before, but I'm too consumed by my ire to dwell on it. I am already failing tonight for reasons I don't quite comprehend, the prince riling me up easier than any stranger has a right to do.

Then again, he's not quite a stranger. I'll be sharing his bed in two nights' time.

That certain knowledge, coupled with his clear disapproval of me, and Einar's unexpected arrival roil in my gut until I know that if I stay in his presence another moment, I will take out my deadly fan and lodge it in his throat.

"No, you didn't think," I interject. "If you'll excuse me, I really shouldn't monopolize your attentions this way." I back away with another graceful curtsy, pretending like we mutually agreed on ending this dance halfway through.

He recovers quickly, bowing in response, a different sort of frown gracing his mouth now. I barely manage to maneuver off the dance floor before he is swarmed by waiting courtiers.

Take him, I want to tell them. *I don't want this anyway.* Any of it.

CHAPTER THIRTY-SIX
AIKA

*J*head straight for the throng of women throwing themselves at the newly widowed king. I try to remind myself they have little more choice in their futures than I do, but it's hard when they're practically fondling him.

The chalyx — Khijhana, lets out a growl. The women scatter, and I feel my lips trying to tilt ever so slightly upward.

I think I might grow to like the beast, as my sister apparently did. I wonder if it misses her.

Did something in Jokith at least love her in an uncomplicated way?

The women aren't deterred for long, so I take my chance to address the king.

"Cousin," I say loudly. "How nice to see you here. Out of mourning." Which is hypocritical coming from me, but I can't seem to help myself.

"Lady Aika." He inclines his head in acknowledgement, a spark of amusement in his eyes. "My wife was such a fan of events such as these. I thought it would do her memory honor to attend."

Liar. But this time, he doesn't even appear to be trying.

"A dance?" He offers his arm before I can say anything in response.

Not about to miss a chance to get some answers, I take the proffered arm and let him lead me out to the dance floor. Khijhana stays behind, though her face looks almost... sulky. She fixes her teal gaze on one of the many couples on the dance floor, placing her giant head on her paws.

Neither of us speaks until we are at the outskirts of the ballroom floor, the music swelling up around us and a steady hum of conversation to help conceal our voices.

I catch a whiff of jasmine, and something in me breaks just a little bit more.

"Did you dance with Zaina like this?" I can't explain my need to know if they were close, to understand a little bit more of how she spent the last months of her life.

Did she dance?

Was she happy?

His brow furrows.

"No," he says quietly. "We never had the time."

"Really?" I don't bother to keep the sarcasm from my tone. "Even though she *loved* events such as these?"

He looks like he either wants to laugh or throw something. "What would you have me say?"

I take a breath and lean into the next few steps of the dance before responding in a quieter tone.

"Is the truth so much to ask?" Another bit of hypocrisy, but we're talking about my sister, and I'm exhausted of the lies.

"That Zaina only barely tolerated social functions?" he responds without hesitation, raising his eyebrows.

"It's a good place to start," I allow.

He spins me in time with the music, matching the pace of the other dancers on the floor. I wait to ask my next question until I'm close to him again.

"Why are you here? To secure a new bride?" Accusation coats my tone, and I don't bother to conceal it.

"No." His lip curls in disgust, his abhorrence of the idea evident even with the rest of his face obscured by the lupine mask.

"Then why?" I demand.

Einar looses a breath, his unnaturally blue eyes boring into mine.

"To talk to you, actually," he says.

That gives me pause. And no small amount of suspicion.

"About what?" I ask.

"About Zaina. I thought you might share some things about her with me, and I got the feeling your... stepmother would prefer not to be confronted by the painful memories."

I nearly snort. Either Mother played her part very well or Einar is being extremely gracious.

"Why do you want to hear about her?" I raise an eyebrow.

"I did care about her. She was my wife." There's an edge to his voice, but what it means, I can't decipher.

"Consort," I correct.

He looks to the ceiling as though it holds answers. "Worry not. She already gave me hell for that one."

There is affection in his tone now, and I am close to believing it, but...

"I'll tell you something then, if you answer a question of mine first."

I don't imagine the rueful grin that passes over his face.

"It's easy to see you were sisters," he mutters.

I suck in a breath. No one has ever compared me to Zai in a positive way.

Not just that, but he didn't say, "she considered you sisters." He said, "you were sisters." What exactly did she tell him? What does he know?

And was that a slip, or a deliberately leading comment?

He gestures for me to go on, but I'm still taken aback enough that instead of thinking about what I really want to know, I blurt out the first question that comes to mind.

"Did you bury her?"

"What?" All traces of amusement vanish from his features, and he misses a step in the dance.

"Her body," I whisper. "Did you bury it?"

"I — no." He belatedly recovers himself. "The ground in Jokith is too hard, too frozen. We burn our dead."

I blink furiously, digesting this new information. In Corentin, only criminals and plague carriers are burned. Even the bodies in the slums get the honor of a proper burial.

"So, let me get this straight." I try to remain calm even though my blood is thundering in my veins. "She was set on fire by a dragon while she was alive, and then you took her body, and you... burned what was left of it?"

Something feels off about this, for someone who claims to have almost loved her, even if it was the custom. Or maybe it's only that I can't bear the idea that *that* was her fate, my beautiful sister, to be burned twice.

I examine Einar closely, honing in on his split second of hesitation.

"There was a pyre at her funeral."

"That isn't what I asked." I'm not sure why this matters to me or why I'm pushing. All I know is that something is not making sense. "Don't think I haven't noticed the way you fail to answer questions. Don't think I will be the only one who notices."

The warning pops out unbidden, but I am beginning to suspect that he's covering something up for Zaina's sake. Maybe I was right, and she went in that cave to die. Maybe he knows that, too, and is preserving her memory by hiding it.

For that matter, maybe there was nothing left of her to bury, and he doesn't want to admit it.

Either way, if I notice a discrepancy, Mother sure as stars will, too.

He turns me again, and I step closer when I spin back around so I can speak in an even lower tone.

"Did you burn her body?" The words are barely a whisper.

"Yes!" he hisses out. "I burned it."

Lie.

I shake my head softly, as much in frustration as sadness. Because he's lying, and it's going to get him killed the same way it did my sister.

"You claim you cared for her, then you refer to her remains as an 'it.'" I give him a moment to ponder that before finishing. "The things you say don't add up. I don't know what you're lying about, but I intend to find out. You'd just better hope I'm the only one."

He peers at me like he's trying to decipher the

meaning behind my words, and I force my features into a bland neutrality.

Neither of us speaks for the rest of the dance.

He doesn't bother asking whatever it was he wanted to know.

*T*he ballroom sparkles in opulence, but it looks garish after the comfortable practicality of Jokith. The lighting is dim, as I predicted it would be, making it even easier for me to blend into the background or duck between the swaying couples.

As much as I underplayed my fear of Madame discovering me, just the thought of being in the same room with her fills me with icy, relentless dread.

I take a deep breath, forcibly slowing my heartbeat as I observe the room. A gaggle of women surrounds my husband, one of them going so far as to put her hands on him. Fury burns through me, and Khijhana growls.

It doesn't help that we haven't spoken since our argument, aside from exchanging a few sparse words about our plan. Though he had returned early enough last night, Einar had found every excuse he could to be elsewhere today, having breakfast and lunch with the king.

I woke up to a box with my costume and a note. *As requested, I procured a costume for* Helga *in case* Helga *has still not changed her mind about risking her own life and our entire plan.*

And now the stubborn arse is standing around getting fawned over when he's supposed to be talking to my sister. Khijhana bares her teeth, picking up on my frustration, and I urge myself to calm down.

Taking a deep breath, I scan the room for anyone roughly Madame's height and build in an ostentatious costume, but she doesn't seem to be here.

The only reason I could see her missing this is if she's hiding from Einar. The thought bolsters me, the idea that we have even this small bit of power over her.

I do see why Einar hasn't yet spoken to Aika when I spot her standing out like a very sore thumb in a bejeweled monstrosity of a mask. At least, I assume it's her, since the costume screams *Madame*. Besides, she's nearly the shortest person in the room.

Then, she does something that erases the very last vestiges of my doubt. No one else in the world would stalk away from the prince mid-dance at his own ball.

Oh, Aika.

She has never been one for subtleties, and I have to wonder if this was all a part of her plan. Though, judging by the way the prince stares after her, perhaps it's working.

"Oh, another kitten, come out to play." A voice behind me interrupts my thoughts. "Here kitty, kitty."

I spin to see a young lord dressed as a bull, complete with a golden nose ring.

It's tempting to pull out my knife and show him exactly what I think of being beckoned, but Einar is pulling the dragon who is probably Aika onto the dance floor.

The condescending lordling might just be useful.

I beam at him, batting my eyelashes while I hold my hand out as if he's already asked me to dance. He puffs out his chest, strutting while he leads me to the floor, and I only barely manage to keep my lip from curling.

Still, at least he's easy enough to move around, even if I do have to push his hand firmly up my back more than once. I'm dancing near Einar within seconds, close enough to hear what is definitely my sister's voice, though it's thick with a posh accent.

"The things you say don't add up," she says. "I don't know what you're lying about, but I intend to find out. You'd just better hope I'm the only one."

She's either warning Einar or threatening him.

She darts a glance over her shoulder, and I hide my face in my partner's chest, prompting him to get far too comfortable. I sincerely hope Einar is not paying attention, lest that temper of his gets the better of him.

It's hard to believe this used to be my life, dancing and flirting and letting men paw at me while I simpered and listened for information after I poisoned their drinks with truth serum.

The lord's hand latches on to my wrist as he spins me, and my vision swirls for a fraction of a second.

Manacles on my wrist.

Warm, sticky breath on my face.

A sharp-edged blade sliding along my skin.

I force my feet to complete the turn, and my partner releases me.

Once Madame is gone, I will never have to tolerate unwanted hands on me again. I bolster myself with the thought, ignoring the crawling of my skin while I finish out the dance to avoid causing a scene.

It's easier to focus with more distance between myself and the overly touchy lord, as this part of the dance allows. The more I ponder Aika's words, the more certain I am that it was a warning rather than a threat. She didn't have to tell Einar she suspected him, but she did.

More than that, she delivered a warning against Madame, something I'm not sure she's ever thought of doing before.

The song comes to an end without either of them saying anything else, and my partner tightens his hold on me like he expects another dance.

"Thank you for the dance, but I'm afraid I'm parched now."

I spin on my heel and maneuver through the crowded dance floor, but I'm only halfway across when a calloused finger slides along my skin. I consider subtly going for my knife, but a deep voice sounds in my ear, tugging at things low in my abdomen.

"Dance with me," Einar growls.

It's more of a demand than a request, and I huff out an irritable breath.

"What will people think?" I half-heartedly argue under my breath, grinning at the courtiers coming to approach my husband, or trying to, though I suspect it looks more like baring my teeth.

"Nothing as bad as they will think if I murder the man who had his hands on you," he says in a barely audible voice, extending his hand to me.

I raise my eyebrows, even though he can't see them behind my mask, then take his hand.

The music picks up again, this time with me in his arms. Even with everything unspoken between us, being this close to him makes me feel... easier. Like I can breathe.

"Well, if that's grounds for murdering, there are quite a few women here who won't live to see tomorrow," I respond.

He chuckles, the sound reverberating from his chest to mine. "At least you didn't let Khijhana eat them."

"Yet."

He spins me away from him and brings me back in even closer than before.

I think about his words yesterday. *You say that like it's a fate worse than death.*

Lifting my mouth closer to his ear, I allow a small bit of teasing to enter my tone. "This is by no means worse than death."

He gives me a wry look, and I continue in a more serious vein. "But it could have been. And I would have had no choice but to stay."

He dips his chin, a muscle ticking in his strong jaw. "I understand. And for what it's worth, I don't want you to have to choose, but the reality is that there will be times you do. That's what being a ruler is."

"That's what it is, to *you*." I amend his statement for him.

"That's what it is to everyone," he continues before I can interrupt, even as I'm glaring at him. "Fortunately for you, this is not one of those times. I agree that we should tell her the truth, sooner than later."

In typical Einar fashion, that was nothing close to an apology. Then again, these aren't issues that are going to be resolved in a night, and the middle of a crowded ball-room is hardly the ideal place to discuss them.

I shake my head a little, letting it go. For now.

Einar and I have had no end of arguments in our time together, but this is the first time we've danced.

Even Madame can't take that from me.

CHAPTER THIRTY-EIGHT
AIKA

I pluck two unflavored sakes off a passing tray, one in each hand, and down them in quick succession. They're bland, and I wrinkle my nose.

"Could you bring me cinnamon sake instead?" I ask the manservant, placing the empty cups on his tray.

He gives me a deep incline of his head and disappears into the crowd while I resist the urge to steal the whiskey from the lord standing next to me.

My head aches from the weight of the jeweled mask, and I'm still reeling from my dance with the king... from everything he knows and from the things I saw swirling in his eyes when he referenced my sister.

Even if he was lying for half of it.

Thinking of Zaina tonight is not conducive to staying in one piece, though, and falling apart has cost me enough as it is. Damian's face looms in my mind.

Hell, it still might cost me everything.

Unfortunately, walking away from Einar has me heading back toward the prince, reminding me that, once again, I have let my emotions get the better of me. If that half dance is all he and I share tonight, Mother will hear of it.

And she will punish me.

When the next dance ends, I slip my way through the ladies to the front, one of the few advantages of my size.

While most of his face is hidden behind his mask, something in his expression shifts when our eyes meet. The set of his jaw changes from the polite grin he gives the courtiers to something a little more genuine.

He steps closer to me, lowering his voice. "Willing to risk another dance with the boorish prince, Lady Aika?"

I soften a bit at his self-deprecating words, in spite of myself. Then again, maybe that's the aftereffects of the sake making this evening a bit more bearable. Still, at least he can acknowledge what an arse he is.

Though, his outward impression of intimacy does little to endear me to the surrounding ladies, judging by their expressions. I suppose I should get used to it, since they'll only hate me more when this is over and I've "won."

"I should get them in while I still can," I allow, my tone dry. "After all, I doubt you'll recognize me tomorrow, what with one courtier being so very indistinguishable from the next."

A low laugh rumbles out of him. He holds out his arm for me, and I take it, allowing him to sweep me toward the middle of the dance floor.

"I suppose it's been a night for mistakes, then, because I was clearly erroneous in assuming there was a courtier in the world like you." From the warm amusement in his tone, it's clear he knows his flattery is over the top and is unconcerned by it.

Still, I can't help the sincere smile that pulls at the

corners of my mouth. I could almost believe that he doesn't hate the idea of marrying me. He turns me in his arms, clearing his throat as I face him once more.

"Which still pales in comparison to the other error, of course." There is a genuine apology in his tone now. "You would think that losing someone would make you more considerate of another person's grief, but it seems so often to go the other way."

I think of the things my grief for Zaina has propelled me into doing, and I can't disagree.

Neither can I judge.

Maybe his flattery is fake, and maybe he's only looking for an accessory to sit prettily by his side while he rules one day, but it isn't like my motives are any better than his.

In fact, they're probably far worse.

Whether it's the unexpected stab of guilt that accompanies that thought, or the strange kinship I feel with him in this moment, something leads me to being more honest than I usually would be.

"When I found out Zaina died," I stop, realizing it's the first time I've said those words out loud.

My hand clenches around the prince's. He surprises me by squeezing gently back, pulling me a bit closer to him.

It's a good thing this dance is slow because I would have certainly stumbled over this unexpected kindness from a veritable stranger. An arrogant prince, at that.

"It took me weeks just to feel like I was human again," I finish my sentence. "Let alone think about anyone else."

It's an uncomfortably true statement, and I'm grateful when he speaks again, stopping my mind from traveling too far down the road of *who* I was the most thoughtless toward.

"You were close." It's not a question, but I nod anyway.

"Like sisters," I choke past the ridiculous lump forming in my throat.

He sways us, still holding on to me firmly like he knows I'm feeling untethered right now. It almost reminds me of—

"It was the same when Louis died," he says. "Except I'm afraid I wasn't nearly as resilient as you are, because it took me a year just to be able to speak his name." A coy grin tilts his mouth up when he says it, but there's grief in his voice that resonates with my own.

Except that the pain of losing his brother was directly caused by the woman who orchestrated our marriage. Though it wasn't my fault, I didn't kill him, I still feel the edges of guilt creeping in all around me.

I grasp around for anything else to talk about besides the gaping hole where my sister used to be and all the people Mother sacrificed to get where she is now.

"Look at us, almost being civil to one another." My mouth manages some imitation of a smile. "Perhaps marriage wouldn't be the worst thing in the world, though I can see why you were sad to pass over such inviting prospects."

I incline my head to where a lady dressed in a black gown with an owl mask is not so subtly yanking the neckline of her dress down, revealing admittedly impressive assets.

"Well, if that's the hand I'm dealt…" Francis lets out a deep chuckle.

His mouth pulls up into the first real grin he's given me, revealing the smallest hint of a dimple.

Warmth spreads through my body, and warning bells clang in my head. I've been so caught up in the bizarre turn of events of this entire evening, so off-footed by the prince's unanticipated conversation, that I have been entirely blind.

The room spins off kilter.

That chuckle. The smirk and the dimple.

The offhand reference to a card game.

The way I can already read the minute changes to an expression with very, very few tells.

My hand loosens around his, my fingers automatically moving against the rough patches evident even through the silk of my gloves.

Callouses. On a prince's hand. Surely, that isn't the norm.

"I was only joking," he offers, like he senses something is bothering me, and I feel so unconscionably stupid for not recognizing that voice before.

But the accent is different, and I never expected to find him here.

Every part of me wants to deny what my mind has already figured out, so I subtly maneuver my steps until we are dancing in the brightest lit part of the room.

Emerald eyes twinkle down at me in wry amusement — eye drops, just like mine, could change the color, but the shape is familiar, even if the sentiment is so at odds with the emotion they held the last time I saw them.

I stop breathing.

Remy.

The prince is Remy.

Remy is the prince.

And I am in deep, deep trouble.

"*I* need to sit down for a moment," I blurt out to a bewildered prince.

Remy. Whoever the hell he is.

It isn't a lie, either. My knees are no longer interested in keeping me upright.

This is an actual nightmare.

"Lady Aika—"

"Truly, it's all right. You should — give another lady a chance to finish this song out." Though, something irrational in me rebels at the notion of him putting his hands on another woman, even though he's not mine.

Even though, apparently, he never was.

That hardly matters now. I shake my head at the direction of my thoughts, heading for one of the tables around the dance floor.

Footsteps follow me, *familiar sands-blasted footsteps,* telling me Remy has no intention of leaving me alone. A servant brings me a tray with the cinnamon sake I requested earlier, and I desperately grab the small cup.

It's halfway to my lips when Remy catches up to me.

He puts a hand on my arm, and the drink sloshes onto my glove, soaking all the way through to my skin.

"It wasn't my intention to offend... again."

"You didn't," I assure him. "I just... had a spell."

It might be one of the least believable lies I've ever told, and Remy's skeptical expression tells me how badly I've sold it. His eyes flit between the small, curved glass in my hand to the stains on my glove.

His hand releases mine, and he steps back, as if he's only just now realizing how close we stand.

"In any case, I seem to have stained your glove."

"It's nothing." I start to move my hand behind my back, but he reaches out to grasp it.

"Please," he says insistently, his tone pitched low enough that our growing crowd of onlookers can't hear him. "We have gotten off to a rocky start. At least let me make up for this much?" There's a teasing glint in his gaze, as though he's trying to put me at ease.

What is in my expression that he feels the need to do that?

That I don't know is a problem in itself. It's my job to know what's reflecting on my features, and usually, one I do quite well.

Whatever it is, I've clearly made enough of a scene. Refusing would only make it worse. Reluctantly, I stretch out my hand.

His fingers go to the hem of my glove, leaving a trail of warmth down my arm as he gently pulls the fabric down. His eyes never leave mine, and the gesture is more intimate than it should be.

"That wasn't so hard, now, was it?" He gives me a half-smirk. "The palace laundresses are magicians. It will be as good as new tomorrow, on my honor."

I don't quite snort, but it's an effort.

What is the honor of a liar and a card shark? I want to ask. *At least I never pretended to have any.*

Once again, he picks up on the shift in my mood, and I wonder how I ever missed that this was Remy, a man who reads people better than anyone I've ever met. I tug my hand back from where he is still holding it in his, and his eyes travel down, widening slightly.

Is he surprised at how easily he touches me? Not likely, when by all accounts, there isn't anyone he *doesn't* touch.

He loosens his grip, and I step away.

Before either of us can speak again, one of the braver ladies moves between us to get his attention. It's the distraction I need to get away from him.

He darts a glance over her shoulder, and I feign a smile in response. As soon as he escorts a lady to the dance floor, I make a run for it. Mother will be furious about my leaving early, but I can't stay in this room another minute.

Besides, I'm not sure I could stomach another dance with the *prince*.

CHAPTER FORTY
AIKA

*M*y mind reels the entire carriage ride home, too many thoughts and emotions swirling around to make sense of.

Remy, who carried me from the scene of my breakdown and shielded me from myself with his arms.

The prince.

A liar.

And what does that mean for last year? All the times he had accused me of being the reason we didn't work out, but he was never in a position to have any kind of a relationship.

Why does that feel like the worst part?

Hadn't I known all along it wasn't real? At least now, I know we were on the same page.

I don't want to think about that anymore, so my mind moves on to my conversation with Einar, which feels stranger by the minute.

He's hiding something, but why lie about what he did with her body? To spare my feelings? Possibly. He is unexpectedly... decent, all things considered.

Did she come to see that, too? Did she see it right away? Was her marriage to him some unexpected fairy tale, or is he playing me?

Maybe he isn't lying at all, and I'm only seeing what I want to see. That thought gives me pause. Do I want to see deceit everywhere? Or am I just better at spotting lies because I am a liar?

I used to believe I was good at judging these things, but Remy has proven me entirely wrong about that.

Remy is Francis...

I ask the driver to take the long way back, but by the time I reach the estate, I still haven't managed to formulate any kind of solid reasoning to stave off Mother's wrath.

One of the servants tells me she's in her room.

It's tempting, so tempting to trudge back to my own chambers, but I know she will hear about what happened tonight and it will look like I have something to hide. So I steel my nerves and school my features into something a little more neutral before heading down the hall.

I remove the dragon mask, looping the sash around my hand while my other fist knocks lightly on her door. For all that I was complaining about the weight of the mask earlier, I miss the shield it offers.

"Enter." Her cold voice floats through the wood, and I reluctantly push the door open.

She's on the balcony, looking out at the waves crashing against the cliffs with an inscrutable expression.

"You're home early." She doesn't turn to face me.

Her tone is a lethal calm, like the beat of silence before a storm descends.

"I had already danced with Prince Francis twice, so I thought it was better to leave with an air of mystery." It's the best I can come up with, and the hard line of her mouth tells me it isn't good enough.

"You thought that with three nights to secure the prince's hand and make it appear as though it wasn't fabricated, your best option was to leave less than two hours into the first one?"

It was more like one and a half, but now hardly seems the time to point that out.

"As I said, we had already danced together twice. Between that and the outfit, I left a strong impression."

"I see." She's still staring out at the sea, her voice even colder than the frigid, churning waters will ever be. "And you danced with no one else?"

"No." I regret the lie as soon as it pops out of my mouth, but I can't quite bring myself to tell her the truth, to be put in the position of telling her what Einar and I talked about.

She rotates slowly to look at me, her expression paralyzing in its eerie emptiness.

"Do you know why I chose you all those years ago?" Her voice is a double-edged sword.

My breaths are too shallow, tendrils of fear creeping up my spine.

"Because I was good at blending in." I repeat back what she's told me more than once.

"No." The word is clipped. "Because even when you were caught, you didn't back down. You didn't backpedal. You never once gave up your lie. But do you remember what I told you that day?"

I'm so numb I can barely form the words. "That lying was a good skill to have, as long as I never again used it on you."

She stares at me, her icy gaze boring straight through me.

"Yes. And in the eight years that followed, I never had to remind you again. Until now."

My heartbeat thunders in my ears and my vision swims. *Air.* I need air, but I can't seem to breathe, let alone form a response or an excuse.

Is she talking about more than my dance? Did Damian tell her about the fires?

If he did, there is no doubt in my mind that this is it for me, that she is finally going to replace me the way she did Rose.

Something in her expression shifts, though, and she lets out a long sigh.

"I have been indulgent with you because I know that you were fond of Zaina."

Loved her, you mean. But I don't dare let that thought show on my face.

"I am sure that the visit from the barbarian she married piqued your curiosity, and I can see why you would be reluctant to admit your distraction on such an important mission." Her unyielding tone is at odds with the sentiment. "That is why I have decided to be lenient, this one time."

She pauses, and I belatedly realize why. Swallowing back the emotions threatening to suffocate me, I give her a deep bow of my head, trying not to actually crumple with relief.

She doesn't know about the fires.

"Thank you, Mother. I am... truly sorry. I was ashamed of letting my emotions get the better of me, when you've devoted so much time to teaching me better than that." I stop before I lay it on too thick, peeking a glance at her.

She appears to be satisfied, though. In fact, she steps closer, placing a hand on my arm.

"It's possible that I was harder on Zaina than I needed to be, at times." Her voice is quiet, her violet eyes brimming with something I can't decipher.

For the first time, it occurs to me that perhaps I'm not the only one who suspects Zaina of maneuvering her way to that cave.

Then Mother shakes off whatever mood overtook her, an icy calm defining her features once more. "But, Aika?"

"Yes, Mother?" I breathe.

"The next time you lie to me will be the last. I have no use for traitors in my family."

"Of course," I say quickly. "It won't happen again."

"I know it won't." Threat laces her tone, and my heart drops into my stomach.

She might be allowing me to live, but there is no chance she will let this go unpunished. It only remains to be seen what form her *discipline* will take this time.

She dismisses me with an imperious wave of her hand.

As soon as I close the door to her room, the panic that has been chasing me all evening, ever since the moment I figured out that Francis was Remy, begins clawing at my chest.

In a sea of tenuous and intangible truths, I am certain of only one thing.

I wish Zaina was here.

CHAPTER FORTY-ONE
ZAINA

*T*he bell is on its fourth and final toll when I reluctantly abandon any hope of sleep.

Which isn't unusual. Since I woke up trapped in my childhood nightmare, sleep has proven to be an elusive prey.

Tonight, my mind refuses to stop analyzing all the reasons Aika may have fled the ball, and what Madame might be doing to her as punishment.

She probably wouldn't ruin her mission by killing Aika, but the things she can do to a person are far worse than death. When the images assaulting me in the dark become too much, I make my way into the main part of the suites, trying not to wake Einar.

Khijhana follows, right on my heels.

A teapot hangs from an iron bar, just close enough to the dwindling hearth to stay warm. The sight soothes something inside me, knowing that Helga or Gunnar took the time to set it up for me.

I'm pouring myself a lightly steaming cup when the front door swings open.

My heart leaps into my throat, but Khijhana's lack of reaction has it calming down before Helga comes into view.

She doesn't comment before she goes to the small bedroom to wake her brother for his shift. She stands watchfully until he emerges, bleary-eyed but alert, to stand guard in the hall.

Once he shuts the door behind him, Helga surprises me by returning to the sitting room instead of heading to bed. She sinks gracefully into one of the chairs, her porcelain features not showing a single sign of fatigue after a night on guard duty.

"You're worried about your sister?" she asks me in Jokithan.

At least she doesn't bother to pretend she and Gunnar can't hear my heated conversations with Einar.

"Always." I let out a wry laugh, but it isn't fooling either of us.

"Is she like you?"

It's an interesting question, and I open my mouth to say *no*, when I reconsider it. Aika and I aren't alike, but we aren't precisely different, either. Two girls taken in by a monster, trained relentlessly and tortured sporadically and exposed to the worst things life has to offer.

"In some ways," I allow. "I suppose it depends on what you mean by that."

Helga meets my eyes directly. "She is a fighter?"

"She's very skilled," I confirm.

Helga hesitates before taking a breath to speak. "Gunnar and I were the same age when our parents died, but he seemed younger to me then. He was smaller, not as strong. I find sometimes that image never really left me. Even now, I forget he can protect himself."

I picture the tall, strong man who rivals Einar in his fighting ability, who required Einar and me both to subdue him when he was poisoned into believing we were the enemy, and I almost laugh.

But I hear what she's saying, and what she isn't.

I let my mind wander back to Aika the day she arrived, skinny and half-starved, covered in fleas. It was only a couple of weeks after Rose died, and all I could see was another victim for Madame to torture and use against me.

"That girl doesn't belong here," I tell Madame.

Frustration laces my tone, and the girl narrows her onyx eyes at me.

"The Girl has a name," she spits. "It's Aika."

"It doesn't matter," I tell her.

She doesn't understand why I don't want her here, why she would be better off anywhere else in the world, why my treating her as anything close to a sister ends badly for both of us.

I spin away from her, walking on soft, even footsteps to my room so that Madame doesn't punish me for insolence. The only reason she didn't already is she's still putting on a show for the girl, but I'm fair game in the privacy of my room.

When the doorknob turns, though, it's Mel's gentle hands maneuvering it. She sits at my desk, her face far graver than any eight-year-old's has the right to be, and scratches out a quick note.

It's not her fault.

"That won't matter," I say bitterly. "It won't save her any more than it did Rose."

The weeks go by, and the new girl is excelling at her training. I see the way Madame's eyes glint when she appraises her, already calculating the various unseemly ways she could be useful.

I find the girl sitting on the rails of the balcony, uncon-

cerned with the way she towers above the churning sea and jagged rocks below. Would that be a quick death, I wonder, kinder than the one Madame gave Rose?

"Girl," I call softly so I don't startle her into falling. "It's not too late to leave, you know. You could find a different home."

She startles me, springing backward with lightning speed and kicking my feet out from under me. I'm about to flip her when I feel the cold steel of a blade at my throat.

She isn't as skilled as I am, not yet, but the tiny girl has overpowered me with the sheer force of her nerve.

"This is my home now. And my name is Aika." Tears sparkle in her eyes, something I haven't seen in the worst, most painful moments of our training.

And I realize that even if it winds up being the death of us both, I can no sooner keep myself from caring about this girl than I could waltz off and leave Mel.

"All right," I say softly. "Aika, then."

Helga's questions sound in my head again, but this time I hear them differently.

I think about the way I walked willingly to that dragon's cave, ready to accept my fate.

Then I think about Aika. Madame aptly named her when she called her "The Flame." She is untamable, relentless, and incapable of backing down.

"She's not like me," I tell Helga.

For the first time since my sister left the ballroom, I take a full, deep breath, because I knew who Aika was far before she learned to wield a weapon.

"She *is* a fighter." Now, we just need to make her understand who the enemy truly is.

CHAPTER FORTY-TWO
EINAR

The bed is empty when I wake up.

That isn't unusual. It shouldn't fill me with panic, but I can't seem to stop my mind from drifting to the first night I awoke to find her gone, and the hellish hours that followed.

I creep into the sitting room to find Zaina on the sofa, sipping a cup of tea. She looks up when I enter, her features tightening at whatever she sees on mine.

I smooth my expression out, even if it is a heartbeat too late. "I'm surprised you didn't go after your sister." I'm not entirely joking.

"I wouldn't have left without telling you." Zaina's tone is too neutral to be casual.

I notice she doesn't bother to say she wouldn't have left at all, just that she would have done me the courtesy of telling me. I suppose that's something.

Sighing, I sink next to her on the sofa. "Why didn't you?"

Part of me hopes she'll say she knew it wasn't worth

the risk. It's a feeble hope, and one she quashes with her response.

"Because I'm trying to trust her to take care of it." That comment is definitely pointed.

I'm debating responding when she clears her throat. "Tomorrow will be our last chance to talk to her before the wedding, but we shouldn't tell her in a room full of people. So, I'll stay in the suites, and you can bring her here."

I raise my eyebrows, wondering if I heard her correctly, and she shoots me a sideways glance. "Khijhana was distracted by me yesterday, and I want her focused on protecting you."

"Even though a ball is hardly a matter of life and death?" I parrot her words back to her, and she scowls.

"After what I saw of Aika yesterday, I wouldn't be so sure."

CHAPTER FORTY-THREE
AIKA

*I*t's another sleepless night.

I can't tell how long I've been staring out the window. Long enough for the stars to shift in the sky and for the moon to ebb away. Long enough that I can see a glimmer of light over the horizon and know that dawn isn't far off.

And still, sleep is out of reach.

How? How is any of this possible?

I close my eyes against the sound of the waves crashing in the distance. If I believed in fate, I would be convinced someone was playing with mine. Perhaps, they are punishing me the way I have deserved for far too long.

The slight quiver in my hand returns, and I try to massage it away. Pulling the fur blanket tighter around my shoulders, I rest my head against the window frame and try to imagine a scenario where any of this will end without death.

I come up empty.

I can't marry him.

But neither do I have a way out of this.

Tradition dictates that the prince announces his choice of bride on the third night of the masquerade. The announcement is binding and followed immediately by the wedding ceremony. If I can keep him from realizing who I am for that long, he will have no choice but to marry me.

Then, we can spend the rest of our lives hating each other.

As furious as I am with Remy, I don't love the idea of tricking anyone into marriage, but I suspect it will be better than the alternative. Walking away from this and letting Mother get her information from him in a more creative way.

After she's finished with me, that is.

My chest tightens, and I reach over to pour myself a dram of whiskey.

I suspect that she doesn't plan for the prince to live a very long life, once she gets whatever it is she wants from this arrangement. If I see this through, though, maybe I can convince her that he is useful.

Or hide him, if it comes to that.

As soon as I think it, I hear how ridiculous it sounds. No one hides from *Madame.*

I drain my glass in one fluid motion, willing the familiar burn to soothe my rapidly fraying nerves. It doesn't work.

There is no way out of this. For either of us.

🔥

Breakfast and lunch are delivered to my room, a message from Mother that this is where I should remain until tonight. The stretches and exercises that clear my head each morning, do nothing to help me now. My mind is still running in furious circles with all of the information from last night.

Maybe I won't need to worry about marrying Remy. Maybe she will kill me after all.

But the hours pass, and I'm still alive.

When the maids arrive with everything to prepare me for tonight's ball, they are as plucky as usual, and I'm left to wonder if I have been misreading the situation.

I've been sitting here, waiting for the other shoe to drop, but maybe it won't. At least, not until I finish the job.

In under an hour, my hair has been pinned up and interspersed with braids and rosettes with baby's breath tucked in here and there.

My makeup is softer than it was last night, with a dusting of blue and white paint on my eyes. My eyes are morphed again, this time with sapphire drops, long lashes that extend further at the corners and a pale blue shimmering gloss on my lips.

The fair lapis fabric of tonight's dress is far preferable to last night's gown, actually allowing me to breathe. As soon as they slip the dress over my head, they attach something to the back and secure the mask to my face.

The mask is an artwork of metal and jewels with various shades of silver and blues and wings attached to the right side to match the ones on my back.

It's an artful take on a luna moth. Unique enough to catch attention, but far more subdued than last night's ensemble.

"Almost perfect." Mother's voice pulls me from my self-examination.

"Mother." I turn to greet her. It doesn't escape my

notice that last night, she had declared me perfect, yet she clearly finds me wanting today.

"Ladies, please leave us," she orders.

Once the maids are gone, she stalks closer, one hand holding a small box and the other gesturing for me to sit on the bench at the foot of my bed.

I can't breathe, wondering what level of horror she has concocted in that box.

She opens the lid, and my knees nearly give out with relief.

Shoes.

They're just shoes.

Bolstered by that realization, I ease forward to examine the exquisite, iridescent slippers. My brow furrows, and the expectant expression in Mother's painted features tells me my relief has come far too soon.

I reach out in trepidation, my nail clinking on the heel of the shoe to confirm what I already suspect.

Glass.

Is this a game? Has she strengthened them somehow?

My fingers trace the ridges of the floral shaped crystals on the outside, sliding down the heel. I've never seen anything like them, and I might be tempted to admire them, were it not for the cruel glint in Mother's violet gaze.

Will I be able to stand in these?

"I need you to understand what is at stake, daughter." Her voice lacks all emotion. "You fled the ball in a hurry last night, something else you failed to mention. When I said I wanted all eyes to be on you, be assured that is not what I had in mind."

My stomach hollows, her next words solidifying the apprehension in my gut.

"You see that I have no choice but to correct your path, to keep you from the temptation of running off again."

She leans down in front of me, taking my ankle in her iron grip and sliding one of the slippers onto my foot. All at once, it's like a thousand wasps have swarmed everywhere the shoe touches.

I inhale a deep, slow breath, counting in my head to ward off the pain. My features don't so much as twitch in reaction as she does the same to my other foot.

This doesn't compare to what she trained me for, but it's an effort to remind my body of that.

"Good," she says, and I'm not sure whether she's referring to the shoes themselves or approving of my stoicism. "The burning sensation will wear off, eventually. It's an alchemical reaction to the adhesive on the shoes."

Adhesive?

"And should you decide to run again, you should know that these shoes are designed to break from the inside out. You shouldn't be inclined to waste any of your dances this way, either, least of all on someone who jeopardizes my entire plan."

My stomach turns. "Mother, how will I—"

"I wish it hadn't come to this. I have always valued your obedience," she cuts me off, taking my chin in her hand and gripping tightly. "If you cannot accomplish this simple task, I will no longer have a use for you. And you know what happens to those I have no use for?"

I force myself to nod.

"Good," she says, standing up. "I didn't work this hard to arrange this marriage just to have you ruin it. I expect better from you. Come now, your carriage is waiting."

I wish her words were angry, that there was any emotion in her voice at all, but there isn't. Somehow, that's worse. Taking only a second to secure my fan to my wrist, I follow her out the door on gentle footfalls, cautiously gauging the durability of the slippers.

Each step is a tenuous balance, a metaphor for my entire life, where one wrong move could shatter everything.

CHAPTER FORTY-FOUR
AIKA

I step down from the carriage with all the grace I can muster, careful not to put too much pressure on the glass shoes.

I suppose Mother could have been harsher with her punishment. I should count myself lucky when I could have been made to walk on knives instead.

With a stilted breath, I follow the women in front of me up the stairs. They're all clucking at one another and gossiping about how much time they spent with the prince last night, as if the others hadn't seen. Only one or two of them mention the girl who fled at the beginning of the night.

"What do you think he said to her to make her leave like that?" one of the women in a rabbit mask asks a doe beside her.

"Who knows? Perhaps she offended him. He was nothing but a *perfect* gentleman to me, so she must have brought it on herself."

I roll my eyes and follow just behind them.

Even if Mother didn't have a spy in place to watch my

every move, the gossips would make sure to fill in any gaps for her.

The soles of my feet still burn from the adhesive, but so far, I haven't felt the slightest crack in my shoes. I can handle the burning.

It's the anticipation of when my shoes might break and what damage they might do to my feet that has me on edge.

One of the guards ushers us inside, handing each of us our dance card for the evening. Tonight is more structured after yesterday's introductions.

I flip the card between my fingers, as if that will steady my frazzled nerves, imagining myself at a tavern instead of a castle.

A round of cards is preferable to the gamble I have to make tonight.

The glowing chandeliers beckon us toward the ballroom in an array of blue and silver and purple light, and I follow the group of women around me, far less eager than they are for tonight's festivities.

As soon as I'm in the ballroom, I bow to the royal family before joining the other women lined up on the dance floor. Tension fills the air now that so many of them have danced with Remy and feel their chances improving or slipping away.

What would they think if they knew the whole game was rigged?

The music slows as we wait for him to arrive. It's still another two minutes before he decides to grace us with his presence.

Tonight, when the prince enters, it's hard for me to look away. His onyx suit accented with small, glowing stars fits him better than anything I've ever seen him wear. His mask is a smattering of silver constellations strewn across a black sky.

Of course, we match again, if less obviously this time.

I am the moth to his night sky; though, we couldn't be more ill-suited for one another.

While there is still an undercurrent of fear of him discovering me, it's drowning in the fresh wave of fury that washes over me when I see him here like this.

I search what I can see of his face for signs of who he really is underneath all the lies. If anyone deserves this feeling, it's me, but that doesn't make it any easier to swallow.

He scans the group of courtiers with a bland smile until his gaze lands on me. Something sparks in his eyes, something I can't quite name.

Once again, he chooses me as his first partner for the evening. It's a message the other ladies have no trouble decoding, but something in his narrowed eyes tells me there's more to it than that.

I take his extended arm, following him to the center of the room.

"I must apologize," I begin, but he cuts me off.

"Not at all. Think nothing of it." His tone is off, shifted subtly from yesterday.

Is he upset because I left him? I let it go without asking. If he's giving me an out, I'm going to take it, especially considering the stakes.

"Tonight's costume is rather clever. Did you choose it yourself?" he asks, pulling me flush against his chest, his left hand resting low on my back while he holds my right hand in his.

"My stepmother chose it," I respond. "Though, I must

admit it is rather clever. Look how well we match — again," I add, giving him a tight-lipped smile in return.

A quick glance around reveals couples positioned in a similar manner, though not nearly as close as we are. The ladies who watch us have their mouths parted in a scandalized O.

When I look back up at Remy, there is a smirk planted solidly on his lips. The same smirk I've seen a thousand times over. It's a reminder of who he's always been, even if I allowed myself to forget that in his rare earnest moments.

Part of me can't help but feel natural in his arms, but the larger part wants to knee him in his manhood for wantonly flirting with a stranger.

As far as he knows, anyway.

"That's how I knew it was you. Should I tell you what I intend to wear tomorrow or shall we leave it to fate?" His deep voice rumbles from his chest to mine, and it's an effort to remember that I'm angry at him for lying just as much as I have.

Hypocrite that I am.

"Ah, yes. Let's see what the fates have in store for us." My tone is dry, and I remind myself that I'm supposed to be selling the idea of marriage to Lady Aika, or at least not deterring it.

The music swells, and Remy leads us in the Starlight Dance, a slow, intimate one that I am grateful for, considering my fragile footwear. He glides me across the dance floor, making me feel lighter than air and angrier than a rabid crow.

Get it together.

It's a good thing I'm nimble-footed, or I suspect the shoes would have splintered already. I can hardly make a show of wooing the prince if I'm hobbling, though, and Mother never would have ruined her own plan that way.

She is nothing if not exacting, so it must be possible to keep these more or less intact.

"I'd like to get to know a little bit about you, considering our upcoming nuptials," Remy says smoothly, gently spinning me away from him and pulling me back in, closer than before. If we had danced this close the first time, I would have figured out who he was sooner. The faint, familiar scent of his shaving oil would have given him away.

"What would you like to know?" I ask.

"What do you like to do for fun? We should get an idea of the kinds of... activities we'll be enjoying together." His words are laced with flirtation, and I would stomp on his foot if it wouldn't hurt me far more than it did him.

Instead, I glance up at him through my thick, artificial lashes and pretend to swoon.

"I'm sure there are many things we could enjoy together once we're married, Your Highness," I say in a coy voice that makes me want to stab myself.

Remy's mask shifts upward as he raises his brows at my suggestive tone.

"Indeed. And I am sure there will be plenty of time for that, but I was hoping to have a better understanding of your hobbies," he says, clearing his throat.

I feign a blush, taking the excuse to giggle into his muscled chest. "Of course, my prince."

"Do you like to paint?" he asks after the next spin.

I blink. *Does he actually want to know this*? Hesitantly, I give him the standard polite answer.

"I do, but I need more practice." It's technically true. I do *need* more practice. I just don't care enough to get any.

He nods his head as if he is only barely listening, which leads me to wonder again why he asked.

"How about embroidery?" Is that amusement in his tone? Is he being boring on purpose? "Many of the ladies at court seem to be taken with needlework."

Meticulously torturing a man with a sharp blade counts as needlework, right?

"Sometimes," I allow. "There's always so much to do during the day that I rarely seem to find the time."

Instead of looking disinterested with my banal chatter like I expect him to, his features glint with interest, and I'm left feeling like I've missed out on the joke.

He opens his mouth to ask something else when the music pauses, signaling an end to our dance. He looks up sharply, like he wasn't prepared for the song to be over.

Like he doesn't want it to be, which makes one of us, because I need a moment to clear my head.

Or at least to fetch a couple of drinks.

CHAPTER FORTY-FIVE

AIKA

*R*emy bows at the end of our dance, his eyes refusing to leave mine.

I return the gesture with a curtsy, pulling my dance card from where I had tucked it into my fan, handing it to him to sign.

When his lips part, I wonder if he's about to begin another string of ridiculous questions, but whatever he was planning to say is abruptly cut off.

My dance card is barely within my grasp when a throng of courtiers surround us, clucking at him like hens for their turn to dance. The one with the mouse mask elbows me hard in the ribs, and I resist the urge to return the kindness.

I flip the dance card irritably through my fingers and slide it back into my fan while Remy is accosted by the sea of women. The woman in the doe mask has convinced him that she should have the honor of the next dance, and the others slowly back away from the couple.

My anger with him is tinged with something more traitorous when he pulls her in close for their dance. He's whispering into her ear, but he can't seem to tear his eyes from me.

I should be glad that Mother's plans are working, that I am succeeding in capturing his attention enough to have him seek me out or to watch me while he's with someone else.

But everything is tainted here, with him and with me.

With us.

I turn away and head directly for one of the waiters holding a tray of champagne. Eagerly, I take one and have barely pressed the glass to my mouth when a deep, familiar voice sounds behind me.

"I'll have one as well."

Seven hells.

I take a breath before turning to face him.

"It's lovely to see you again, Lady Delmara," Einar greets me.

"You as well, Your Majesty," I say, dipping into a curtsy, keeping my interactions formal for the sake of whoever is watching.

"May I have this next dance?" he asks, and I nearly spit out my champagne in response.

Swallowing it down, I shake my head in disbelief.

Of course, he would ask after Mother specifically forbade me to dance with him again.

She isn't wrong about appearances, given the number of women throwing themselves at the king and the assumption that Remy had made. Still, I wonder once more if there's something she doesn't want me to know, something I could learn from him.

Then I'm reminded of the burning in my feet and how much we will all pay if my curiosity gets the better of me.

"Forgive me, but I think I need to sit this one out." I give him a terse nod.

"I think you'll want to make an exception." His tone tells me there is more he isn't saying.

But I can't afford to find out what it is. Already, heads are turned in our direction, people taking note of our interaction. Of course. Einar is even more eligible than their precious Prince Francis.

"You don't understand," I say, glancing toward the crowd.

Einar cuts me off. "That's where you're wrong. I think I do understand, more than you'd imagine." He takes a deep breath, morphing his features into something less intent. "What if we grab a drink instead? Surely *no one* would think anything of that."

I study his expression, turning over the curious emphasis of his words in my mind. Regardless, he isn't wrong, and at the moment, we're drawing more attention standing here than we would if we both happened to be at the bar.

"All right. A drink it is." I nod tersely.

He follows me over to the less crowded bar, ordering a vintage scotch while I order yet another cinnamon sake.

He stares ahead as he sips his drink.

"I think it's time that we talked." His face is relaxed, at odds with the tension in his tone.

"I'm not sure it is," I disagree, mindful of anyone trying to listen in on our conversation.

"Not here, but maybe you'll find yourself venturing into my suites again sometime this evening. Maybe you could use the front door this time," he remarks casually.

But it's no casual thing he asks of me, and I sense that he knows that.

ELLE MADISON & ROBIN D. MAHLE

After all, he is aware that I broke into his suites. What else does he know?

"Tempting, but not worth my life," I reply, hiding.

He drains his glass before responding.

"And what about the life of your sister?" he asks, meeting my eyes for the first time since we came to the bar.

My grip tightens around the bladed fan at my wrist, and it's an effort to keep my features neutral with the threat looming over Melodi's life. I slowly turn to face the king, infusing my whispered words with as much venom as I possibly can.

"She has nothing to do with any of this, and if you or anyone else harms a hair on her head, so help me, I will—"

"You misunderstand me, Aika." Einar's words cut me off mid-sentence. "I do not mean Mel any harm."

Mel? Aika? Since when does he feel so familiar with either of us?

His glacial-blue eyes stare back at me with a sincerity that I hadn't expected.

"Then what did you mean?" I demand after a breath.

The music slows to a stop just as he nods, and he looks around the room as if he's searching for someone.

Everyone applauds the latest round of dancers as I wait for Einar's reply, but the next voice I hear isn't his at all.

CHAPTER FORTY-SIX
AIKA

*E*inar steps away as Remy comes closer, placing his hand on the small of my back.

"Forgive me, Your Majesty, but I must insist on this next dance with the lady."

Do I detect a note of jealousy?

"Of course. Thank you for the drink, my lady." The king reluctantly dips his head in a bow to both me and Remy, and there is a promise in his gaze that we will finish our conversation later.

With my head still spinning, I take Remy's hand and follow him away from the bar to one of the far corners of the dance floor.

"Did you miss me already, my prince?" I ask sweetly as I take up my position to begin the next dance.

A dry laugh escapes him.

"Something like that." He sways me to the music.

This dance doesn't involve grand, sweeping motions; it isn't a work of art like the others. This one is for couples to enjoy their time together, to gaze into one another's eyes, sharing secrets and whispered words.

Another one that the ladies are sure to be envious of, not to mention the fact that he sought me out, again, when they have to throw themselves at him in order to be seen.

Remy is quiet for a long moment while the violin swells to a crescendo. I take advantage of the break to replay the conversation with Einar in my head, picking apart each word for every possible way he meant them.

If he wasn't talking about Mel...

"We were cut off before, when I was trying to get to know you better." Remy interrupts my thoughts, his fingers running idly up and down the small of my back.

I suppress a shiver at the familiar touch.

"Yes, I was forced to take turns with the others." I inject a bit of petulance into my voice to conceal my maelstrom of emotions. "I'm looking forward to when I won't have to do that anymore. I never have been very good at sharing."

"No, I can't imagine that you are." Remy's mouth tugs up at the corner.

I'm not sure if I should take that as a compliment or not, so I let it slide all together.

"You know, if I close my eyes, I can almost imagine I'm at this little bar in the mid-sector. It has the same feel, though my company tonight is far better than any I ever found there," he says, continuing to draw half circles on my spine.

The hell it is, arseface.

My next several thoughts collide as I attempt to respond as any young lady from court.

"And do you find yourself in the company of other women at these bars? Or is it more of a gentlemen's club?"

I keep my tone pleasant, though I refuse to look him in the eye.

"There are some women, yes. But none so lovely as you." He lays the compliment on thick. "Mostly, we just play cards together. Do you play?"

"No. I can't say that I'm much one for games," I reply drily.

Remy lets out a small laugh, pulling me in tighter and whispering into my ear.

"Somehow, I very much doubt that." His words are smooth, and it takes everything in me not to react.

"I'm certain the ladies there were quite taken with you, what with having a prince sneaking out to see them," I say, batting my lashes at him while I wonder if I should let Mother plan his death, after all.

"Oh, but they didn't know. I went under the guise of being a guard."

"What a husband I've landed myself," I grit out.

At this point, I'm certain even a demure lady of the court would be aggravated, and I've hardly pretended to be that. "A liar *and* a scoundrel. Tell me, shall I expect those pursuits to continue throughout our joyous union?"

"You do yourself a great disservice, my lady." He holds a hand to his heart in offense. "Any harlots that I may have been with before were dalliances at best, distractions at worse. None so... accomplished as you are." The barest bitter edge coats his tone, and a sneaking suspicion creeps into my mind.

"I assure you," I bite back. "My *accomplishments* are nothing compared to your own."

He purses his lips. "Don't sell yourself short. You really are a standout. One might even say you're *on fire*."

The last two words come out a hiss, and I stumble, my

ankle twisting beneath me in a dance that should be easy. The glass fractures at the instep, and I curse internally.

Remy holds me upright, though his expression is hard, nothing at all like it was yesterday when he was carefully removing my glove.

I meet his gaze, the eyes he hasn't bothered to color tonight, and it's obvious that he knows. All that remains to be seen now is which of us will fold first.

He leans down until I can feel his breath on my ear, giving every outward appearance of intimacy. But there is nothing romantic about what he whispers next.

"Your mask is slipping."

CHAPTER FORTY-SEVEN

AIKA

*R*emy is no one's fool, which, I suppose, makes one of us.

Though his eyes burn with something between fury and resignation, he puts his hand on my wrist and tugs me toward a hallway, though not the one I gesture toward.

I struggle to keep up with his pace and keep the shoes intact, but I'll be damned if I ask him to slow down. Einar's eyes follow us out, his expression inscrutable, but that's a complication I can't deal with right now.

The fractured glass in my shoe pinches my skin with each step we take, becoming nearly as irritating as Remy is. He dismisses the guards in the hallway, waiting until we're completely alone to speak.

"Care to tell me what in the seven hells you're doing here?"

"I would think that's obvious." I shrug, mostly to irritate him.

"And here I thought you said you weren't much one for games. Where is the Lady Aika?"

"I *am* the Lady Aika," I spit back.

Remy's eyes narrow, and he runs a hand through his hair.

"Then who the hell is Gemma?" he asks.

My anger is boiling to the surface now, and I strain to keep my voice low. "I don't know, *Francis*. Who the hell is Remy?"

"I — It —" he splutters, taking a half step backward. "That is not the same thing."

"I'm pretty sure it is."

"No." He sounds more certain now. "No, it isn't because I don't go around murdering people."

We're back to this again.

"Of course not," I scoff. "Because taking out criminals would require you actually getting off your arse to do something about the state of the city instead of just whining about it. You think Madame is responsible for all the crime here? Maybe you should look a bit closer to home."

He bristles at the insult. "I don't think Madame is responsible for all the crime in the city, Gemma. Hell, I'm beginning to think you're responsible for at least half of it."

I roll my eyes. "Meanwhile, you're just responsible for half the bastards born into it."

A noise sounds around the corner, and Remy pulls me farther into the darkened hall. When we're far enough in, he stops, crowding me against the wall.

"Really? You want to put those things in the same category?" His voice is lower than before.

"I'm just saying, you hardly have the moral high ground here." I cross my arms over my chest as if that will somehow put more distance between us.

"I think it's fair to say that just about everyone in that room has the moral high ground over you." He gestures dramatically to the ballroom, then to me. "You torture people and burn them alive."

"Only the ones who deserve it," I mutter.

He lets out a measured breath like he's trying not to yell. "I'm not doing this with you again. I don't have time to argue with you because now I have less than two nights to find a wife."

Panic floods my veins.

I don't relish the idea of a drawn-out death at Mother's hands, or even just weeks of torture in the dungeon.

For that matter, if he refuses to marry me, I doubt seriously Remy will enjoy her methods of forcing his hand. Which she undoubtedly will, as long as I'm around.

"You can't." I throw out a hand to grab him. "We have to get married."

I'm grasping for a reason to give him as his jaw drops in disbelief.

"Are you that desperate for power?" he bites out. "We definitely do not have to get married. I'm sure that when they made this arrangement, my parents didn't know you were the vigilante!"

"Unless you actually do want me to hang, we can't very well tell them now, either." I'm banking on whatever residual mercy he has for me to avoid telling him things that will get us both killed, but he surprises me by shaking his head.

"I'm sure you'll be able to make something up. You're good at that."

Before I can think of a response, he spins around and saunters back to the ballroom. I don't want to follow him yet, not until I have some kind of a plan.

I never get the chance to think of one, though, before a shape materializes from the shadows, and icy dread spreads throughout my body.

Damian.

CHAPTER FORTY-EIGHT

AIKA

*D*amian's smug expression is all the confirmation I need that he heard everything.

My heart plummets to the bottom of my gut, and my vision darkens in the corners. How is it that after years of being the perfect soldier, the perfect *daughter*, I have failed so epically tonight?

If Mother finds out, there will be no getting out of this. No going back.

I grasp around for a lie.

"Shouldn't you be more discreet? Anyone could see you here. Put your mask back on and let's go." I speak with a confidence I've pulled directly from my arse as I attempt to walk past him.

He grabs hold of my arm tightly, forcing me to stop at his side.

"I knew it." His voice is a thousand tiny spiders crawling onto my skin. "This whole time, I knew it was you."

"What are you going on about? Let go of me." I pull away from his grasp.

His fingers only dig in deeper as he tugs me closer to him. Damian shakes his head, a low chuckle escaping his scarred lips.

"Even you can't lie your way out of this. I heard every word." He drags me from the room back out into the dark hallway. "Now, we will hear what Mother has to say about it."

I fight to get away from him and feel the crack in my shoe widen with each strained movement. Any other time, if we had an even playing field, I would have no problem escaping him.

There has to be a way out of this.

Anything would be better than the slow, agonizing death Mother will deal me. *Bloody hell,* she'll probably let Damian do it while she watches, and I have more dignity than to let myself be killed by him.

I'll take my own life first.

"As usual, *Brother*, you don't know what you're talking about. Just let me go and I will explain it all in a way that thick skull of yours can comprehend."

The only response he gives is the back of his hand across my face, sending my mask flying to the floor. I open my fan, spinning back toward him.

My arm sails through the air, slicing the fan across his face and chest, and I try to use his momentary shock to scramble backward in an attempt to regain my footing.

Which is next to impossible thanks to Mother.

A slow grin spreads over his twisted mouth as he darts toward me. Taking up a defensive position, I ready myself for his next attack, but instead of drawing a weapon to fight back, he lunges for me, grabbing me by the waist and pummeling me flat on my back.

My lungs burn for air, but my grip tightens on my fan

as I bring up my arm, running it over his chest and arms before he can stop me.

Damian shows no fear of being cut again as he grabs hold of my arm, pinning it beneath him. *Maybe nothing is scary compared to dragon fire.* He rips the fan from my grasp and chucks it down the hall, far away from us, before standing.

Panic grips me, but I stuff it down, fighting him as he hauls me to my feet.

It doesn't matter that my shoes are breaking around my feet, or that I'm out of weapons. I need to get away from him any way I can. I dig my heels into the rug in an effort to slow him down, but all it does is send shooting pains from my toes all the way up my legs.

My vision swims, but I wrestle to break free.

I refuse to make this easy on him.

His face takes on a murderous expression when I finally slip from his grasp. Then his hands are on my dress, tugging me back to him. The sound of fabric tearing fills the hall as he throws my wings to the ground, grasping for me again.

Wrenching me upright, he hits me hard across the head. The room sways again, but I'm quick to respond with a sharp kick to his groin. My dress is slipping off of my shoulders, and I'm preparing to rip the entire thing off to run away when the cold steel of Damian's blade is at my throat.

He grabs hold of my hair, using it to spin me around to face him, his dagger still at my throat.

"Please keep fighting." His breath is hot on my mouth. "I'd love an excuse to bring you so much more pain."

Instead of responding to him, I react without thinking,

screaming loudly for the guards. He knows how much Mother hates a scene.

Damian's jaw twitches, the only real sign of his agitation, as the sound of boots come running down the hall.

"If they arrest me, I will find a way out." His tone is as eerily calm as ever. "Either way, Mother will hear about this, and there is nowhere you can go that is beyond her reach."

"They're not for you." I spit the words at him, and his eyes widen in the smallest hint of surprise.

The sound of stomping boots round the corner just as Damian slips into the shadows. I whip around to face them and come up short when Lawrence is standing in front of me.

My mind is running on fumes, and I know I don't have long before they will demand answers or leave. There is no scenario I can think of where Damian won't follow me and drag me back to *her*, no way for me to escape him in these wretched shoes.

Lawrence's brows knit together as he glances back and forth between my face, my falling dress, and the mask on the floor.

"Gem—" he begins, taking a hesitant step forward.

"What is the meaning of this?" Einar's voice interrupts from behind the guards as he tries to push his way forward.

Remy is the next to join him, the anger twisting his features replaced by shock when he takes in the blood dripping from my nose and the way my arms do little to conceal my torn dress.

I am practically bare, on display for everyone, and I can't think of a single lie to get me out of this.

So, I settle on the truth.

Before I can think better of it, four impossible words escape my lips.

"I am the vigilante."

The hall goes silent. Lawrence exchanges an alarmed look with Remy, while Einar opens his mouth to speak.

So I talk first, making the decision for all of them.

"I demand to be arrested and face the consequences," I say, holding out my wrists and limping toward the guards.

Under the law, they have no choice but to take me into custody. And under the law, I will have to face the hangman's noose.

Lawrence reluctantly pulls the iron cuffs from his belt and locks them around my wrists, his mahogany eyes boring into mine with grim resignation.

I look away from him, from all of them, before I can regret the most impulsive decision I've ever made.

At least this is a death of my choosing.

CHAPTER FORTY-NINE
AIKA

*M*y mind dances from one thought to the next as the guards drag me down the winding stone steps to the dungeons.

What have I done?

It felt like the right thing to do at the moment. Anything else would have put me at risk of facing Damian or Mother and the brutal wrath she would have undoubtedly brought down on me.

But now...

Every limping step sends my heartbeat racing, and panic is crawling its way up from inside of me, threatening to do me in.

My eyes dart from one guard to the next, wondering how much time it would take to incapacitate them all. I count down the seconds it will take to reach the dungeon floor and start to control my breathing. I need to focus and have a clear plan of attack if I'm going to make this work.

When we reach the bottom step and round the corner just in front of the well-worn entrance of the dungeon, I fight back. It's unexpected, considering that I demanded to be arrested.

So, it takes them a moment to realize what's happening.

The guard to my left goes to his knees in the narrow hallway when I turn on him and quickly strike his chin with the heel of my palm as hard as I can. Another guard approaches from behind, and I throw my elbow into his neck.

He falls back toward the wall, wheezing as the next one makes his move.

This guy hunches down low as if he's going to tackle me to the ground. When he comes running at me, I throw the chain of my cuffs around his neck, using his own momentum against him when my knee connects solidly with his face.

The sound of his nose breaking echoes in the hall, and I ignore the stabbing pain and crunching of glass at my feet.

For a moment, I think I can do this, I've taken half of them out easily, I can take the rest out, too. And where I go from there... I'll figure it out later. Right now, all I know is that I need to get out of this dungeon.

I raise my fists, ready to attack the next guard, when two arms wrap around me in a bruising hold. I thrash my head backward, but all I'm hitting is his chest. The grip around me tightens, as if I'm being strangled by a coiled, hungry snake, but I keep fighting.

I kick my feet at the approaching guard, but it's useless. He stays far enough out of reach that I can't make contact.

Tosser.

When my line of vision starts to blur, I know I've been bested. The dread I felt before only triples.

Finally, it's Lawrence's fuzzy face I see in front of me. He's boldly standing close, as if he's daring me to hit him. My foot twitches, every instinct telling me he's just as much of a threat as the others, but I don't lash out.

Lawrence doesn't order the guard to stand down or ease up. He just waves toward the large metal door ahead.

My body seizes on the way through. This can't be it. A part of me wants to keep fighting, to use whatever I have in me to get out of here, but then I hear Remy's voice, less taunting than it was in real life.

You have to know when to fold, Gemma.

Every ounce of me wants to rebel at the mere notion of giving up, but my body has other plans. I take a wheezing breath as the echo of his words deflates whatever fight was left in me.

Everything goes black, and I faintly register the squeal of rusty hinges. The next thing I know, I'm being thrown into a cell. The snake uncoils around my lungs just before I land hard on the ground.

I can't stop coughing and wheezing long enough to hear what Lawrence is telling the guard.

All I can see is the metal key twisting in the lock, sealing my fate.

It's scarcely been an hour since the guards left, but it feels as if it's been much longer.

The small mattress in the corner is littered with pests, and my skin is already itching with their bites. Between that and the damp chill wafting in from the small, barred window, it would have been nice if my clothes had stayed intact.

And these aren't even the real dungeons, I think bitterly. *These are just the cozy holding cells they keep you in until you're prosecuted.*

I keep track of every sound in the dungeon, waiting for the familiar rhythm of boots in the hall alerting me to the guards. But all I hear is the skittering of a rat across the cold stone floor, the nearly imperceptible sound of a spider weaving a web of silk in the window above me and the slow drip, drip, drip of water from the ceiling.

Still, this is a step up from the alleyways I used to sleep in.

It was raining the night my father decided that parenting wasn't for him, and finding a dry place to sleep on the streets was nearly impossible.

I would have killed for the lice-covered mattress there.

Every day, I wondered if the guards would arrest me for stealing from the vendors at the square, and every night, I worried that the slavers would come for me.

I never imagined that I would demand to be arrested, or that I'd end up engaged to an arse-faced prince, or even that I'd spend my last nights on earth in the royal dungeons.

I sigh and rub my temples.

What have I done?

None of the guards have come back to tell me what's next, maybe because it's obvious. I run a hand over my neck where the hangman's noose will rest and wonder for the hundredth time if damning myself really was the best solution.

Suddenly, Zai's and Mel's warnings about my impetuous nature feel valid.

I hadn't thought it through before. It seemed like my only option in the heat of the moment, but now that my death lingers in the air like a promise, that certainty is feeling a little less solid.

For all the good that knowledge does me now.

CHAPTER FIFTY
AIKA

*T*he minutes slip by in a curious blend of monotony and anxiety before achingly familiar footsteps echo on the stone dungeon floor.

My heartbeat falters. I didn't expect him to come.

When Remy comes into view, illuminated by a few flickering lanterns, his face is filled with a sorrow I've never seen him wear before.

He thrusts something at me through the doors — a pile of clothes. He turns around while I put them on, and I wonder if it's as much to hide his face as to give me privacy.

I carefully guide my shoes through the leggings, setting the slippers he brought me aside. Jealousy is an absurd emotion, given the circumstances. Still, I can't help but wonder which woman's shoes he just happened to have lying around.

"All done," I announce.

He turns around, scanning me briefly.

"Going to take those ridiculous shoes to your grave? Literally." He chokes out a bitter laugh.

"May as well go out in style." I shrug.

I'm not about to admit I am stuck in these sands-forsaken shoes, that I'll be hobbling all the way to the noose in them.

A beat of silence passes.

"What happened after I left the hallway?" he asks.

"Nothing." It's not even a good lie, but I'm too tired to come up with anything better.

"Nothing," he repeats, his tone mocking. "So, you panic about anyone finding out you're the vigilante, then I leave, your dress magically tears itself, and you have an epiphany and decide to turn yourself in?"

He waits for me to respond, but there's nothing I can tell him.

"Do you not understand what's at stake here? My mother has been tearing apart the kingdom trying to find the vigilante, and you come right out and admit to it?"

I notice he doesn't say his father, and I wonder if Mother used her considerable influence with the queen to propel that manhunt.

"Why is she so worried about a criminal who only targets other criminals? It's not as though her precious nobles are at risk."

He lets out an angry breath through his nose. "When the people stop trusting the crown to do justice, crime gets more prevalent everywhere. It puts everyone at risk."

A bitter laugh escapes me. "If the crown is *impotent*, Remy, maybe they should work a little harder to actually stop crime rather than just making it look like they're trying."

"The vigilante is a criminal!" His voice rises on the last word. "Why are you so determined to martyr yourself for the sake of your right to burn people alive?"

"I don't know, Remy," I yell right back. "Why is *the crown* so much more upset over a bunch of dead slavers than the innocent people who were taken? Or maybe I've just missed all the human traders and drug pushers you've taken into custody tonight?"

I make a show of cupping my hands around my mouth and yelling, "Any slavers out there? No?"

Remy shakes his head furiously. "You really want to discuss the shortcomings of *the crown*," he emphasizes the word like he knows I was referring to him, "when you're facing the gallows?"

"If I'm facing the gallows, there will hardly be another time to discuss it." I shrug with all the nonchalance I don't feel.

"This isn't funny, Gemma — Aika — whatever the hell your name is. I can't get you out of this."

"It's Aika," I mutter. "And I didn't ask you to get me out of this."

"So, what, you've just resigned yourself to hanging? Why would you do that?"

Why, indeed?

There's not an answer I can give him that will make this easier on either of us, and I can't quite bring myself to tell him the truth about Mother. He already thinks I'm enough of a monster.

Besides, if I'm out of the picture, her motive for going through Remy is gone. Probably.

If he knows her involvement in this, though, he'll only try to go after her again. Then, she will kill him for sure.

I say nothing about that, instead forcing one corner of my mouth up. "Don't ask questions you don't want the answer to."

His eyes take on a calculating gleam I don't like.

263

"All right, then. I'll make statements instead." Anger still brims under the surface of his tone, but it's tempered now. "Your friend Leila was the Lady Zaina."

I don't so much as twitch a muscle, but my silence is confirmation enough.

"And news of her death came about a month ago." His tone is softer on those words. "Coincidentally, right when the fires began."

I shake my head, less in denial and more because these are conclusions I don't want him reaching. I don't need his understanding or his absolution, not now.

"You said she was like a sister to you."

I still say nothing.

"That you didn't feel human for weeks after her death."

More silence, tinged with anger at the nerve he has bringing up words that weren't even meant for him.

"You're a lady of the court, and I'm going to be king. If I speak on your behalf, my father may have leniency. He may be able to grant you confinement to your estate. Surely, that's better than hanging."

Hah. Right back into Mother's loving embrace.

"Your mother, you mean." It's clear enough she's the one running this show. "And don't bring Zaina into this," I order sharply, not meeting his eyes.

The only thing worse than being tortured by Mother and Damian would be having my grief paraded in front of the world first.

"Damn it, Gem — Aika!" His jaw clenches, frustration and something deeper, something closer to desperation, pinching his perfect features. "Can't you see that I'm trying to save your life here?"

Tears stab at the back of my eyes, and I feel my resolve crumbling at the sound of my name, my real name, on his lips. I can't afford that right now, though, not for either of our sakes.

"No one can save me. I don't even want to be saved," I lie. "The only thing you can do for me now is leave, *Francis.*"

He searches my gaze for several interminable moments, the lines of his face hardening when he sees the resolve in mine.

"My name is Francis Pemberly Remington Cornelius Ashington." He speaks slowly, his tone indecipherable. "But my sisters call me Remy. Especially when they're exasperated, taking turns coming to fetch me from a tavern in town before my mother finds out I'm gone."

My lips part, though I tell myself it doesn't matter, that it never did. "Well, at least something you said was true." My words aren't half as casual as I wish they were.

Remy turns his head to the side, like he's waiting for me to say something else. When I don't, his shoulders fall.

"That's apparently more than I can say for you," he murmurs, turning around.

I search for something to prove him wrong, a single truth to leave him with.

"For what it's worth... cinnamon sake really is my favorite drink."

I rarely lose my temper, and I raise my voice even less frequently. But when Einar tells me my sister was taken by the palace guards, all of my carefully cultivated self-control disappears into a cloud of rage.

"*Sands-blasted hells!* I should have gone tonight." I had been so sure that I could balance cautiousness with protecting her, and I had been wrong.

Now, my sister is in the dungeons.

"You couldn't have fought off a palace full of guards, and you would have revealed yourself trying," Einar counters.

I level a look at him. "I might have been able to stop her, though, from..." I trail off, my fingers going to massage my temples because I'm still not sure what she was playing at.

"There might still be a diplomatic way to handle this. Let me talk to the king."

"There isn't time for that." I fight to keep my voice even. "She won't last the night in that dungeon. Madame would never risk her being interrogated by the palace. If she doesn't manage to capture her to *extract information* herself, she will damned sure make sure no one else can."

Another tense beat of silence goes by before I speak again.

"I'll just have to go get her." How hard could it be, defeating at least half a dozen guards and sneaking out the most notorious criminal in all of Corentin?

"By yourself?" Einar is already poised to argue, and I cut him off.

We don't have time to rehash everything we've been fighting about right now.

"I know how you feel about me risking our mission with Madame to save one single, reckless person," I say, remembering the way he had refused to pull a petal early to try to find a cure for Sigrid because of the risk of ruining it for everyone else.

There are icicles in his eyes when they meet mine. "I understand your need to save one person, however reckless. What I don't understand is how readily you put everyone else at risk for that. Even now. Even after everything."

My head pounds as I take in his expression, his posture, and the bitter resignation in his tone. Before I can manage any kind of cohesive response, there's a knock on the door.

Einar and I exchange a wary glance as Helga's voice sounds out.

"The Crown Prince Francis to see His Majesty."

Einar clears his throat, giving me a moment to slip into the bedroom before he calls, "See him in."

I watch through the same crack in the door I had used

for Aika as a tall man with a lean, muscular frame strides through the door.

A very familiar man.

Sands. Blasted. Hells.

Einar gestures for Francis — Remy to sit, but Remy shakes his head, pacing the perimeter of the room instead. His eyes flit from the two glasses on the coffee table to where Khijhana currently stands, not between him and Einar, but between him and the door I'm standing behind.

Just when I thought this situation couldn't get any more complicated.

His inscrutable expression gives nothing away, though. Not that it ever has, as far as I remember.

"I'm here about the Lady Aika," he announces.

"I assumed as much." Einar's game face rivals Remy's.

It could be carved from marble for all the expression he shows, but his shoulders are taut with tension.

Remy studies him. "She will hang for this, confessing in front of witnesses and refusing to defend herself."

My heart drops into my stomach. *The hell she will. Not while I'm alive to stop it.*

Einar's jaw clenches, and Remy's gaze homes in on it.

"If you have any designs on helping her escape," he continues in a lofty tone. "You'd be best to rid yourself of them now."

Einar opens his mouth to argue, but Remy barrels on. "Even though the outer guards will be otherwise engaged at the midnight toll of the bell, leaving only two at the interior, you can't think that a man so conspicuous as yourself could have a chance at escaping with her."

I narrow my eyes, and my husband mirrors the expression.

"Indeed," is all Einar replies. "Whereas a man such as yourself…"

"Will be dancing in full view of the queen's watchful guard." Remy's features don't twitch, but he looks around ostensibly and speaks in a louder voice. "If only there were someone who she might trust, someone who was good at hiding."

Given that Remy was an accomplished enough liar to fool even my sister, I have no reason to trust him now. Still, I saw the way he carried her tenderly from the site of her fire, and he's clearly kept her secret this long.

More importantly, I have no way of getting her out without him.

With a resigned sigh, I heave the door to the room open. It's just another risk I have to take.

I only hope Einar sees it that way.

CHAPTER FIFTY-TWO
AIKA

innamon sake really is my favorite drink?
I massage my temples as I go over the conversation in my mind. That was the only truth I could think to give him, and the look of disappointment on his face said more than his silence.

I wrap my arms around my body, trying to disappear into the loose-fitting tunic Remy gave me. Anything to stave off the cold, damp air. I'm resting my head against the stone wall when a faint footstep draws my attention.

Several seconds later, Damian's slimy voice slithers into my ears.

His feral grin is wide as he takes in the image of me in this cell.

"Welcome, Damian. Do make yourself at home. May I offer you a refreshment? Perhaps some mold from the wall? Or a dribble of rat piss?"

"Appreciated, but I'm satisfied just seeing you here, like this," he begins. "What did you really think you would accomplish by landing yourself in the king's dungeons? Do you truly think you have escaped Mother's wrath?"

I shrug in response, crossing my arms and not deigning to let him know that very thought has been plaguing me since I announced I was the vigilante.

Damian shakes his head and drags his knuckles across the metal bars of my cell. "This won't go very far, Sister. Mother will interfere before the king or queen hear a word of this. She wouldn't dare let you off as easily as a royal proclamation and a public hanging." He tsks. "That would be too quick."

"Are you sure about that, Damian? I think your time in the dungeons has made you confused. How do you know that Mother will believe you?"

The corner of his mouth creeps upward, tugging at the scars on his face as he continues as if I haven't spoken.

"I can't wait to tell her about your little lover's quarrel with the prince. What do you think she'll make of that?" He tilts his head to the side, examining me and the reaction I hadn't meant to let slip. "I'm certain she'll be very interested to know what sort of understanding the two of you had behind her back. How long do you think it will take him to break?"

Dread pools in my stomach, and I try to steady my breathing. There is no response I can give that won't put Remy in more danger.

I had thought that if I was removed from the equation, Remy would be safe. But now... If Damian reports on whatever he thinks he saw, I know that she will kill Remy. Especially if she thinks I have betrayed her to him.

I try to view the situation from Damian's eyes, and it isn't good.

If she thinks for one second that Remy knew anything about me, my time as the vigilante, or about her...

Fear rakes its icy tendrils down my back, and I want to be sick.

Damian must sense this, because his eyes widen along with his demented grin until the sound of a metal door squeaks on its hinges.

"I'll be back for you later," he whispers and disappears around the corner.

The sound of boots stomping toward me barely drowns out the sound of a door closing in the direction Damian left. I sit up straighter when one of the guards brings me a plate of stale bread and a cup of water.

He grimaces as he shoves it through the hole in the door toward me.

I stumble in my broken shoes and reach out to catch the cup on instinct, barely saving the water from spilling everywhere. Too many years of going hungry taught me not to look a gift horse in the mouth.

"You're really the one who set all of those fires?" the guard asks.

"I'm not in the mood. Go play with someone else," I respond, narrowing my eyes at him.

"I don't believe it. Little thing like you... Who helped you?" His eyes inch down from my head to my feet.

"If I tell you, you have to promise not to say a word." He leans in conspiratorially. "It was your mother," I whisper with a wink.

The guard's features go rigid, and he scoffs. When he finally leaves and I'm certain no one else is planning a visit, my shoulders relax, and I place my head in my hands, rocking back and forth.

With tossers like him on the royal guard, no wonder crime runs rampant in the city. Squeezing my eyes shut, my mind runs through a million questions and a million what-ifs, but one thing stands out among the rest.

How in the bloody hell am I going to save Remy?

*R*emy is playing a dangerous game, but I haven't quite deciphered to what end.

Still, this is our best chance at getting Aika out, even if I do get the feeling he doesn't trust me any more than I trust him.

What I can't quite figure out is why he cares enough to risk this when he was willing to walk away from my sister before.

I mull that over as I slip through the back entrance of the dungeon. The solitary guard that was stationed there was easy enough to take out without too much of a struggle, but I don't envy the headache he'll have when he wakes up.

I sneak down the damp halls and past the sleeping prisoners until I find the right cell block.

Another guard is walking down the middle of the hall, checking on each cell as he goes. I creep up behind him and press the chloroform kerchief to his mouth just like the last one, easing him against the wall when his body goes limp.

Removing his keys as quietly as I can, I stalk down to the seventh cell on the right and brace myself for Aika's reaction to seeing me. Alive.

Her eyes lock on to mine, emotions flitting through them faster than I can identify.

"Bloody hell." She lets out a huff of air, shaking her head. "I knew you weren't dead."

I'm not sure what I was expecting her to say, but it certainly wasn't that. Part of me is grateful that she seems like the same Aika I've always known. Another part wants to yell at her.

Of course, she's posturing when I had to sneak down here to drag her out of the sands-blasted dungeons.

I slide the hood off of my cloak and sort through the keys for the one that matches her lock.

"You really couldn't manage to stay out of trouble in the handful of months I was gone?" If she wants to play it this way, then I will. *For now.*

Aika snorts and throws herself back onto the disgusting mattress, as if she's quite at home in the rat-infested dungeons.

"Well, since you were busy *playing dead* and driving our dear mother mad with grief, I've been a little busy."

There it is, the anger I've been expecting.

"So I see," I reply with a sigh.

When I find the correct key, I unlock the obnoxiously squeaky door to usher her out. As I step closer, I register the bruises on her face and knuckles and undoubtedly the rest of her body, judging by the way she winces as she stands.

I clear my throat and meet her eyes again.

"Dare I even ask how you landed yourself in a dungeon?"

Instead of telling me what really happened, why she outed herself, she rolls her eyes and shrugs me off.

"Could you possibly save your highhanded attitude for *after* we escape the castle?" Her features are neutral, but there is an edge to her voice.

"Would you rather I leave you here, then?"

"Nope." She pushes past me, with all of the confidence of someone who hasn't been arrested for mass murder. "I'm far too busy to relax in these royal suites, but thank you."

"Indeed," I say, shaking my head.

Then, she says something that sucks all of the air from the room.

"Speaking of being busy... I do hope you plan to stop by and visit our brother now that you're back. Maybe the sight of you returned from the dead will finally do the tosser in."

I freeze. My heart. My lungs. Everything stops as I wait for her to laugh, to tell me she was joking.

"What do you mean, our *brother*?" I hold out a hand to stop her from going any further, practically hissing the words at her. "Damian is dead."

"No," she says, shaking her head. "He's scarred and even more disgusting than usual, but I can assure you, Damian is very much alive."

Her last five words echo all around and through me.

I want to believe she's lying, getting me back for not telling her I was alive, but I realize this is what's been bugging me about the alchemist, how he knew about the dragon.

Damian told him.

This could change everything. If he suspects that I'm alive, all of our plans are at risk. If he—

There is no time to process that, though. I steady myself, shaking off the images of him in flames, the memories of his hands on me in the dragon's cave, but his threats echo in my head.

"Where is he?" I ask. "Is he with Mel?"

"Not yet. She's at the Chateau, safe... for now," Aika says darkly. She doesn't look confused, only grim, and I wonder if Madame has told her about *giving* Mel to Damian. Bile rises in my throat.

We can't do anything about that right now, though, or ever if we don't get out of here.

"That will have to wait," I say on an exhale. "Our time is nearly up."

Aika dips her head once, already in action mode. Something in the simple gesture is comforting.

I almost forgot how seamlessly we work together with the efficiency and skill that nearly a decade of training has granted us. My sister follows more slowly than usual, but her soundless steps in those ridiculous shoes are a testament to her skill.

For the first time since leaving Jokith to embark on this insane, overwhelming mission, I feel an unexpected surge of hope, sharpened by the barest edge of vengeance.

When Madame took children and molded them into weapons, I wonder if it ever occurred to her that they could be her undoing.

CHAPTER FIFTY-FOUR
AIKA

"You're sure you can't remember what the adhesive smelled like? Was it sweet? Or did it sort of burn your nose?" Zaina asks in the same practical tone she's always used when she's figuring something out.

She appears to be content to pretend the past four months haven't happened at all.

Meanwhile, I'm propped up on a bed in the royal guest suites while the Jokithan King and my dead sister examine my glass-encased feet. The tenuous walk from the dungeons was not kind to the gruesome footwear, and now shards of glass bite into my flesh at every turn.

"It didn't have a smell," I tell her again, with no small amount of aggravation in my tone. "It just burned like hell when she put them on."

"Everything has a smell. Just think, Aika. If we don't get these off soon, you're going to get an infection." She eyes the blood creeping its way down the long fractures in the thick glass. "That is, if you don't have one already. We need to nail down what she used if we have a chance of counteracting it."

"Well, it will be a real travesty if my foot gets infected before Mother tortures me to death," I snap. "I hardly think this is our most important concern."

I still have to figure out how to warn Remy, how to hide him from Mother.

"You're so right." Zaina's words drip with sarcasm. "You should be escaping right now. Tell me, how quickly do you think you'll be able to hobble your way out of her reach on those?"

I seethe. "Maybe I wouldn't have to worry about hobbling out of her reach at all if you hadn't let me believe you were dead for a month!"

The room goes silent, even Khijhana stopping in her tracks.

My sister's expression is somewhere between guilt and frustration. "It wasn't like I could go around announcing it."

"Yet you had no problem telling people you had known a handful of weeks?" The pressure is building, the culmination of everything that transpired over the past few months crashing down on me.

All that grief and rage and pain, for what?

"That's... complicated. You don't understand—" Zaina's overly reasonable tone rips cleanly through whatever fragile thread of calm I'm clinging to.

"No, *you* don't understand!" I cut her off. "Mother knows that I set fire to her empire, something that only happened, by the way, because I was drowning in guilt and grief over your pretend death."

She rears back like I slapped her, but I don't stop. I can't.

"You know what she does to traitors. While you've clearly moved on with your cushy new life and your new family and your pet, I have *no one*."

"If—" Zaina tries to break in, but I barrel over her.

"Mel is stuck on the island. I'm not Zaina enough for Mother, or Gemma enough for Remy, or Rose enough for you, and I am right back where I started eight years ago, with no home. I have nothing. Because of you." Bitterness chokes me. "I knew you hated me, at first, but I honestly thought that somewhere along the way, we became family. But family doesn't do this to each other. Family doesn't *abandon* each other."

Zaina's perfect features freeze, her lips paused halfway through whatever she was trying to say. It may be the first time I've seen her at a loss for words.

"I never hated you," she whispers. "I just... didn't want you there, so soon after Rose."

My breath catches in my throat. Somehow, that hurts worse.

"Well, I'm sorry I could never be your precious Rose."

I pause, and Zaina just shakes her head mutely.

"Why did you bother coming back, then?" I gesture to the room outside. "You clearly have everything you want, so why didn't you just do us all a favor and stay dead?"

"I very nearly *did* die." Disbelief coats her features, and she's sure as hell found her voice now. She's as close to yelling as I've ever heard her. "I suppose then you would have gotten everything you want, too."

I open my mouth to respond when Einar steps forward.

"We'll all be dead if the two of you continue to alert the entire castle to your presence." A muscle ticks in his jaw. "Since the two people in this room who have been *trained* for stealth seem to have forgotten that they are supposed to be in hiding," he pauses and looks at Zaina for a pointed moment, "I'm going to suggest that we all get some rest and deal with this in the morning."

Zaina's cheeks color, with shame or anger, I can't be sure. I'm not even sure which one I'm feeling at this point.

"Fine," she says, giving a terse nod before leaving.

"You'll be safe here for the night," Einar tells me before he turns to follow her.

I snort. He's either lying to himself or he's lying to me.

There is nowhere safe from *Madame*.

I sink onto the edge of the plush mattress in the room I share with Einar, massaging my temples while he lies next to me with his arms folded behind his head.

For all his impression of nonchalance, the muscles in his biceps are clenched.

We haven't spoken more than a handful of words since I revealed myself to Remy, since I went to retrieve Aika on nothing more than his dubious word.

I am the one to shatter the deafening silence now, but not in the way I intend to. "I can't believe that after everything, she thinks I hate her."

My voice is more raw than I mean it to be, and Einar shifts.

"She doesn't think you hate her." He sighs. "She just doesn't think she's important to you."

Something in his tone feels pointed and I snap my head up, observing the tight set of his mouth and his carefully guarded eyes. "A feeling you sympathize with."

It's only a guess, but I know I'm right when he doesn't

argue. My chest tightens, and traitorous tears prick behind my eyes.

"The ability to compartmentalize is a good quality in a queen."

I scoff softly. "Just not in a person."

He holds my gaze. "No. In a person, too, when it's necessary. You just don't always shut it off, the way you focus on a single thing to the exclusion of everything else around you."

Everyone, he means.

"You think it's my fault that she wishes I was still dead." My voice wobbles on the last word, and I abruptly close my mouth.

"She didn't mean that."

"You can't know that," I whisper.

"I can," he argues. "I saw her grief firsthand. And besides, I know another woman who sometimes says hateful things when she's backed into a corner."

I turn to look at him, forcing a tiny smirk to my mouth.

"Well, I would say I'm sorry, but queens don't apologize."

He shakes his head, a huff of laughter escaping his lips, though it doesn't quite reach his eyes.

"Nonetheless, I accept." He stretches his arm out in an invitation and a truce.

I nestle against his chest, allowing myself to take solace in the way my head rises and falls with each of his breaths.

"As you know," he says abruptly. "Kings don't apologize, either."

"But if they did?" I ask.

"If they did, I might explain that even though I pushed

for us to do this, even though I have nothing but faith in your brilliant mind and your deadly skill, it would still be hard for me when you put yourself on the line so recklessly, every time."

"I know you're worried about our plan, but now that Aika — and hell, Remy, are around, you could still take on Madame if something happened to me. Our people would still be safe." I trace the lines of his chest and abs with feather-light fingertips.

He lets out a long, exasperated breath. "It's not just about the plan, Zaina. Don't you understand that it will never be easy for me to watch the person I love most in the world put her life on the line? And that it's markedly harder when you treat your life like it's expendable, like," he pauses, his jaw clenching. "Like, if you died, it wouldn't kill me, too."

My breath catches in my throat, and I swallow.

The last thing I want to do is hurt him. I wish I could tell him that it changes everything, that I will be more careful, more safe, more... something, but all I can give him is the truth.

My truth.

"I love you too, Einar. That's why I will do anything to see us on the other side of this."

"I know." He tightens his hold on me, like he can keep me in this world through sheer force of his will. "That's what I'm afraid of."

CHAPTER FIFTY-SIX

AIKA

*M*other's voice resounds in my dreams.

'You see that I have no choice but to correct your path.' Her hand tenderly cups my cheek. *'To keep you from the temptation of running off again.'*

A match flares to life in a glass bottle, and her hand pulls away.

She touches the match against each of my feet. Over and over again, they catch fire. She laughs as I hold back my tears.

One useless daughter is enough.

Her face is carved from stone as she stares down at me.

I call out to Remy, but he shakes his head bitterly and walks away.

I try to speak, to explain or lie or say anything at all, but no sound escapes my lips. Then, the sequence starts again, and again.

Until the gentle scent of jasmine comes in to drive it all away.

At last, I have peace.

❦

I sit up before my eyes are all the way open, already on alert in the unfamiliar room. A hand on my wrist stops me before I can draw my weapon.

"It's all right. You're safe. It's just me." Zaina's voice feels almost as surreal as the dreams did. Something in the way she says the words makes me think it isn't the first time.

Nodding, I pull my hand away and sink back to my pillow. My sister retracts her hand as well, settling back on her side of the mattress where she must have slept last night.

We lay in silence for another few minutes. Our argument from earlier invades the air between us like the gas from one of Mother's poisons, sucking the oxygen from the room.

I turn over on my side to face her, taking in the very real and very alive version of her that I never imagined seeing again. I'm grappling with what to say, with whether I should speak at all, when she breaks the silence.

"You're right, you know. You were never going to be Rose." Her quiet tone feels louder than it should in the dimly lit room.

Hearing her confirm what I've felt for years stabs sharper than the glass on the tender flesh of my feet, but she isn't finished.

"I loved Rose, but she couldn't survive Madame's world, and you could. You have. But... I didn't want you to have to." She takes a breath. "It wasn't that I hated you. It was that I didn't want that life for you. Any of it. But we *are* family, Aika. You and me and Mel." She trails off for a minute, her voice weaker when she speaks again. "That's why I did all of this."

The silence between us stretches out like a dense, impenetrable fog. I don't quite know how to respond to her, so I eventually settle for asking a question.

"Are you ever going to tell me what *all of this* is?"

She takes another deep breath, and I can feel her hesitation before she speaks again. "I want to eliminate Madame. I want us all to be free of her."

I wait for the shock to settle in, but it never does. On some subconscious level, I knew that already. What else could this have been about?

On the heels of that thought, another dawns on me, one that pierces into me, sharper and more painful than the glass in my shoes.

"And that's why you didn't tell me," I rasp. "You weren't sure if I would take your side over hers."

The uncertain look on Zaina's face tells me I've guessed correctly. I can't pretend not to understand on some level. With Mother, everything is murky. Even now, I'm not sure Zaina was wrong to doubt me.

Would I have taken her side?

Will I now?

Could I betray the woman who gave me everything I have? Who gave me my sisters? Escaping Madame for the time being is a world apart from actively trying to take her down.

I see the reflection of my thoughts in Zaina's golden eyes, and I know one thing for certain.

"For what it's worth," I tell her. "I don't wish you had stayed dead."

Recognizing the mess we're both in has siphoned the

ELLE MADISON & ROBIN D. MAHLE

anger from me, at least for now, leaving a trail of fatigue in its wake.

She nods but doesn't respond.

"You were wrong, though," I add. "I may not have gone directly against her, but I never would have thrown you in her line of fire, either."

"I understand that now," Zaina says.

She doesn't comment on my vague use of the past tense, and she doesn't ask me what I will do now.

Another beat of silence passes before I speak again. "You can't honestly think that you can beat her, though, Zai. I'm not sure anyone can."

"Maybe not any one person." The way she says that makes me think back to the way Mother hid from Einar, and I wonder all over again what their history is.

Zaina doesn't give me time to dwell on it before she moves on, though. "It hardly matters right now. First, we need to get you out of this mess."

She sounds so confident, just like she always has. In spite of myself, in spite of all the mixed feelings I have about my sister, the barest edge of hope creeps in. "How exactly do you plan on doing that?"

She takes a deep, fortifying breath, like she knows I won't like what she says next. "We might have a contact here in the palace."

"Who?" My tone is sharper than I mean it to be.

"Remy."

I suck in a sharp breath. When he left the dungeons, I was sure I would never see him again. And now he was helping me. *Why?* His *mercy* again?

Zaina raises her eyebrows. "Or are we calling him Francis now?"

"You noticed that, too," I say sardonically.

"It was rather hard to miss when he showed up in our suites." At my confused look, she expounds. "How did you think I got you out of the dungeons so easily?"

"Oh, so he was in the very select group of people you felt needed to know you were alive," I can't help but say.

She shoots me a sideways glance. "Yes, well, I was rather limited in my options when you wound up in the dungeons."

"Regardless, Remy — we're *not* calling him Francis — is the one who needs help from me."

"So, we'll need to find a way to hide you both…" Zaina doesn't look alarmed, only contemplative. "Einar may have some ideas."

"Is the great and all-knowing Zaina actually going to ask someone for help?" I mock.

She opens her mouth to respond, but she doesn't get a chance to say a word before she's interrupted by a heavy, authoritative knock at the door. My heart seizes in my chest.

Someone knows I'm here.

*M*y heartbeat thunders in my ears.

Is it the guard? Mother?

Belatedly, I notice Zaina shows no hint of surprise. She only shuffles closer to the door to get a peek. I narrow my eyes at her and gingerly follow suit, though I immediately regret it. My feet are throbbing, and each step is agony.

"May I help you?" The male Jokithan guard asks in the main room, but it isn't Remy's voice that answers.

"His Royal Highness Prince Francis has sent me with a missive for this room," Lawrence says in a clipped tone. "I was instructed to give it to the king."

The sound of heavy footfalls makes its way toward the door until Einar is visible. He reaches out and takes the note from Lawrence, flipping it over so that Zai and I can see the name "Gemma" written on the envelope.

"He sent this along with the note," Lawrence adds and Einar opens the door a little wider to grab the box being passed to him.

What's going on?

Einar inclines his head, and there's a pause before Lawrence clears his throat pointedly.

"Yes?" Einar asks.

"His Royal Highness is risking a great deal." His voice quiets. "I wouldn't like to see that backfire on him."

"Of course," Einar says after a beat, his shoulders going tense.

"Oh, forgive me, I nearly forgot one more thing. Lady Delmara has arrived at the palace," Lawrence says, as if it's an afterthought and not the kind of news that has my blood freezing in my veins.

Einar only nods and closes the door.

Zaina helps me limp toward the sofa in the main room to sit, propping my feet up on the small table before standing to walk around.

"Do you think she's here to see the queen about having you removed from the dungeons?" she asks.

"For the pretense of it, maybe," I respond. "Damian promised to come back for me last night. He will have told her I was gone by now."

Einar's eyes widen, and he looks to Zaina for confirmation. My sister barely pauses in her pacing of the room to give him a curt nod. He curses under his breath, crossing the room to hand me the note from Lawrence.

I tear open the envelope to find that Remy's brief words take up very little space on the royal stationery.

I have a way out. Meet me in the ballroom at the fifth bell.
-R

. . .

Zaina reads the note over my head. She goes to open the box that accompanied it.

"I don't plan on taking whatever 'out' he's offering. The stupid boy doesn't understand the danger he's in." I rub a hand over my face. "But I suppose if this is the only way to warn him, then so be it."

Zaina's brow furrows. She reaches into the box and pulls out an ombre mask that fades from white to gray to black.

Then, she removes a swath of black fabric and holds it up for me to see.

"How thoughtful of him to secure a dress for me to wear to his wedding." I try to make a joke, but it falls flat. "I wonder if he'll choose Lady Trinity for her lovely… assets."

Zaina's features soften slightly as she examines the gown. "Well, at least he knows your color."

"Or he thinks I'll be in mourning," I respond bitterly.

I can't help but watch my sister as she helps to prepare me for the evening. Do normal families do this? Discuss dresses? Choose jewelry for one another? Help with their hair?

I try to imagine growing up in a home where Mel and Zai and I were allowed those moments of sisterhood but come up short.

I push the thoughts aside, concentrating instead on the gown Remy sent over. As much as I hate to admit it, it's beautiful. The tip of the corseted strapless bodice is a pale, shimmering silver, darkening gradually down the dress until the hemline is a charcoal so dark, it's almost black.

Surprisingly, the dress is almost short enough for me, though Zaina has to yank the corset ribbons all the way through to make it tight enough around my bust. I take a half step to avoid tumbling over, realizing my mistake too late.

My vision darkens and pain lances through my entire body.

Zaina notices the way my cheeks pale and quickly calls Helga over, asking her to bring one of the vials on the desk.

"This isn't like the one Madame makes," she explains, handing it to me. "It won't actually heal you, but it will help somewhat numb the pain for a few hours," she says, taking the vial back after I've downed it. "Let's just hope whatever he has planned won't take longer than that."

"Let's just hope I can warn him and get him out of the ballroom before Mother has anything to say about it," I reply, and Zaina nods her head.

It's another hour before I'm ready, but with the makeup that Zaina brought and Helga's surprising skill with hair, I won't stand out in the ballroom.

My bruises are covered, and my bloody feet are mostly concealed by the full skirts of the gown.

"Never would have guessed I was a prisoner in the royal dungeons last night, would you?" I ask, admiring the black paint Zaina used for my lips.

She rolls her eyes as she does the finishing touches on her own hair.

"You're welcome," she responds and comes to stand next to me.

Both of us are nearly unrecognizable, masked and disguised and ready for tonight. I think again about what we might have been like in different circumstances, ones where we weren't constantly in competition with one another.

Zaina reaches out to squeeze my hand, and I wonder if she's thinking the same thing.

I wonder if we'll ever get the chance to do things differently.

I head to the ballroom, picking my way precariously down the grand staircase on my ruined feet.

As with the first two nights, I'm alone, but tonight is the first time it doesn't feel that way.

Einar is already in the ballroom, keeping an eye on things ahead of time, and Zaina is coming right behind me.

Then there's Remy, who is allegedly meeting me there.

I've given up trying to figure out what his game is, if he has an actual plan and why he wouldn't just tell me.

I'm certainly not thinking about who he's going to marry tonight and whether he'll enjoy being wrapped in her arms in the days or hours before Mother swoops in to exact her vengeance.

I am so actively *not* wondering about those things that I allow myself to become distracted for a fraction of a heartbeat.

And it is still too long.

I should have guessed she might be in the great hall,

might be making her exit just as the ball was beginning. I *would* have, were it not for the distraction of Remy and Zaina and a thousand other things.

But I didn't, so I am caught entirely off guard when Mother turns a corner not fifteen feet from where I'm standing at the bottom of the staircase.

She is flawless, not a single hair or stray thread out of place, no sign that she might be in any distress. Her features are as cold and unyielding as ever, but her golden eyes sparkle with suppressed rage.

Even the lords and ladies who know her as nothing more than Lady Delmara give her a wide berth as she glides through the spacious entryway.

I force myself to keep moving, since remaining frozen on the spot will only draw attention. Worse yet, I have to walk toward Mother in order to go in the direction of the arriving courtiers.

She can't see me, I assure myself. Zaina has done her job well, and the mask is not one Mother has any cause to look twice at.

This is what I do. I blend in.

Picking up my skirts, I move to fuse myself with a group of ladies, but they quickly outpace me. Still, Mother doesn't so much as glance in my direction as I slip past her. I risk looking back over my shoulder a few times, but she seems to be moving along.

I am close, so close to breathing a sigh of relief when she pauses. Her head turns, focusing on the spot I was standing in a moment ago.

That's when I see it.

Blood.

Tiny, crimson droplets like a trail of macabre breadcrumbs on the pristine marble floor, every one of them leading directly to me.

She turns in slow motion, like she is fighting against her own disbelief, and I will myself to walk faster. Faster, and quieter. I am only steps from the ballroom where it will be easier to lose her, and I don't dare look back again.

Fear clenches every muscle in my body, but somehow, I keep moving.

The bell tolls, low rings reverberating throughout the castle, nearly loud enough to drown out the sound of my rapidly beating heart.

It's time, and I am nearly there. A throng of courtiers loiters just inside the doors of the ballroom, perfect for me to lose myself in.

My breaths are coming shallow when they deign to come at all, but by the third toll of the massive bronze bell, I am stepping into the ballroom. Remy stands waiting in the center of the room, unmasked and not bothering to hide his expression for a change.

So I see the way he anxiously searches the doorway, and I see the moment his eyes land on me.

I take a step toward him, but a hand closes around my elbow, slowly yanking me backward.

Clang.

The fourth toll of the bell. Everything slows down. I see Einar's eyes widening in horror, his hand stretching toward the axe on his back, for all the good it would do.

Khijhana takes a step forward, her lips curling up to show her massive teeth.

The powerful grip succeeds in spinning me all the way around, and my eyes land on Mother. Her dark face pales with fury, her features carved into a snarl more feral than anything the chalyx could ever hope to achieve.

301

Zaina is frozen several steps behind Mother, her lips parted underneath a glittering tiger mask.

Clang.

The silence after the fifth toll is deafening. I search for anything that might preserve my life in this moment. Anything that might keep Zaina and Einar and even Khijhana from throwing their lot in with mine.

I open my mouth to speak, to come up with a lie big enough and believable enough to get me out of this, when another voice sounds out instead, louder and closer than I expect it to be.

"I choose Lady Aika Delmara as my bride."

THE END

Dying to know how Madame feels about that ending?
Don't miss out on what happens next.
Pre-order your copy of Book Four on Amazon now!

Of Thieves and Shadows
Coming March 2022

A MESSAGE FROM US

Want free books? If you email us a link or photo of your review, you'll have a chance to be on our exclusive Street Team, with access to our entire backlog and advance copies of our upcoming works for free!

Email: whiskeyandwillow.llc@gmail.com

Authors, in particular indie authors like us, make their living on reviews, so if you enjoyed this book please take a moment to let people know on Amazon, Goodreads, and/or BookBub!

Social media gushing is also encouraged and very appreciated

Remember, reviews don't have to be long. They can be as simple as an: 'I loved it!' or: 'Not my cup of tea...' So please, take a moment to let us know what you think. We depend on your feedback!

ELLE'S ACKNOWLEDGMENTS

My mind is still spinning that we're actually at the point where we can finally share Aika with all of you. Robin and I truly thought no one could be more difficult than Zaina, but we were wrong. So, so wrong…

But, now that we're here and it's done, I can honestly say I'm proud of how this story went. Sure, there were other directions we could have gone in, other decisions our characters could have made, but this feels the most authentic and I truly hope you all enjoy and appreciate Aika's journey.

Now, onto all of the people who made this moment possible!

Robin… You are the best co-author and friend I could ask for. You spent months in the trenches with me, battling everything that tried to make this story not happen, and engaging in all of the 'side quests' we went on with first, second and third iterations of these wily characters. And we did it, we actually did it and made it out on the other side, mostly in one piece. Thank you for your drive and focus and the energy you poured into this book (especially all those line-edits) you are the cog that keeps our writing machine going, and I'm so grateful to be on your team <3

Brianna, there aren't enough words to express how much your help and insight means to us. You are a priceless gem and without you, there would be no cohesion in Aika's story AT ALL. Thank you for your endless well of support and for always rooting for us.

Jamie!! You beautiful ray of whiskey sunshine, you!!

I adore every fiber of your being. We couldn't do any of this without you, nor do we ever plan to. Thank you for your patience with us, your constant support, and your continued tolerance for my misuse of commas. Love you!

Kate, you are our last line of defense, our knight in shining armor, our favorite kiwi. Thank you for your late night messages, your memes, your hilarious banter and mostly, for the way you catch all of our inconsistencies and those blasted few typos determined to make their way into the final version of our books. You're the best.

Lissa, you have been with us from the beginning and your constant support means the world to us. Thank you for your kind messages of encouragement and just for being you <3

To our **Alphas**, **Betas** and **Grunions**; what in the world would we do without you girls??? Robin and I are so fortunate to have each of you on our team and to have such enthusiastic friends and readers!! Thank you for all of your help with this story, for helping us smooth over those rougher edges and for loving Remy even when he had the charm of a dishcloth.

To our **Drifters and Wanderers** and our **ARC team**,

thank you all for believing in us and supporting us while we spent far too long in our writing cave for this one.

And finally, **to my hubby**. Thank you for your patience while I spent countless hours obsessing over and struggling with this story. Thank you for your support and your encouragement to keep going, and thank you for being the best husband and father to our children. I love you more than pink Starbursts.

ROBIN'S ACKNOWLEDGEMENTS

As always, my first thank you goes to my bestie co-author. Aika threw us for a loop, and then another, and more after that. I probably would have given up somewhere around the third iteration of her plot without you there suffering alongside me. I'm so glad we're in this together for the ups and downs, and I'm so excited with who Aika turned out to be and the story that eventually unraveled.

Our Alpha Team, our Grunions, our Final Beta team, you guys are the absolute best! Seriously, your attention to detail and the time you took to provide us feedback, your cheers and your critiques, made the editing process easier and more solid than it's ever been. I am eternally grateful to each of you!

Jamie, no one will ever be as patient with us and our ridiculousness as you are. It's hard to believe this is the 12th book you've edited for me!!! Thank you for always making sure we put out the best version of things instead of the mess we send your way to begin with.

Brianna, I'm not actually sure this book would have happened at all without you. Certainly it wouldn't have happened on time or been half as cohesive. I don't know of anyone in the world that does what you do half as well as you do it, and I count myself so fortunate to have found you so early in my career. You make writing so much less stressful for us!!

Kate, even if you sucked as an editor, I would love you for our late night ridiculous anime and cat and "prescription" messages. But on top of that, you go and root every last inconsistency and beat our novels into submission like a boss. Thank you!

Lissa, you remind me every week why I do this, and you don't know what that means to me!

To our awesome readers, our Drifters and Wanderers, our Street Team, and everyone who has reached out to us about our story, you are the reason we write and the reason we are able to keep writing. Thank you so much for your continued support!

And finally, to the love of my life and the best dad my babies could have asked for. Thank you for getting me into the world of writing and giving me the support I needed to stay here. Most importantly, thank you for listening to me talk for days on end about a plot hole that's not really a plot hole until I've worked through it in my head. You are my favorite favorite husband.

ABOUT THE AUTHOR

Elle and Robin can usually be found on road trips around the US haunting taco-festivals and taking selfies with unsuspecting Spice Girls impersonators. They have a combined PH.D in Faery Folklore and keep a romance advice column under a British pen-name for raccoons. The two have a rare blood type made up solely of red wine, and can only write books while under the influence of the full moon. Between the two of them they've created a small army of insatiable humans and when not wrangling them into their cages, they can be seen dancing jigs and sacrificing brownie batter the pits of their stomachs. And somewhere between their busy schedules, they still find time to create worlds and put them into books.

Made in United States
Orlando, FL
05 January 2024

42146589R00200